THE FINAL SAVE

BROKEN CIRCLE DUOLOGY
BOOK TWO

DAN BLAKELY

For the one who left the flower

Arbelon
Veilspen
Wastelands
Wayfe
Thessian Sea
Salile
Comstock
Trosten
Asmenson

ountains
The Great Forest
Veydris
Devendor
Felderwin
Anryneach Divide
Swain

1

—————

FALLOUT

EVERYTHING WAS WHITE.

Not with the warmth of Arbelon—this was something colder. Sterile. It pressed into Thane's skull like static and wouldn't let go. It was the kind of white that hummed behind your eyes, buzzing in your jaw, too clean to be real.

Then the memories came. The glow of the Heart, the figure inside, the face he couldn't unsee.

But how? It was impossible.

He blinked once, then again, and the light resolved— slow and mean—into a ceiling. A grid of tiles. Flat, featureless, and artificial.

Shapes followed. A monitor, glowing green in the corner of his vision. Tubes at his wrist. Clear plastic. A needle held in place with pale white tape. He couldn't just feel the IV, the *idea* of it lingered like it had always been there.

His skin was damp. Sheets stuck to him. Antiseptic burned behind his nose, pungent and stale.

Then voices came. Muffled and small, like someone had stuffed cotton between him and the world.

"His vitals are finally stabilizing," a male voice said, flat and clinical.

Then another voice, softer, and familiar, edged with desperation.

"He just… collapsed," his mom said.

Thane didn't react, but the sound of her voice cut through the static. Not because it was loud, it was because it was *hers*. It was too much, too soon, and kept his eyes on the ceiling.

Footsteps. Shoes whispering across linoleum, and the click of a clipboard. He could hear someone writing—each pen stroke louder than it should've been.

"I don't even know how he was playing. I took the damn cord," his mom said, like she was trying to convince herself. "I *took* it."

Another pause. Her breath caught.

"The headset's fried. Sparks were coming out the side when I found him."

A third voice joined, measured and steady. It was Dr. Hughes. He was always calm in the worst moments, which made it dig deeper into Thane.

"We'll need to monitor him closely. The disease is progressing rapidly." He paused. "Honestly, Jane, I'm less concerned about the game than the cognitive spiral. If he continues to confuse it with reality…"

Reality.

The word stuck in Thane's mind like a splinter. His breath caught, small and tight, but it was enough.

His mother gasped. "Thane?" She was close now, her voice barely holding together. "Sweetheart, can you hear me?"

He didn't answer. Didn't move. Just stared at the IV like it was some kind of restraint. One of his hands twitched under the sheet—half a spasm, half a reflex. His other curled into a fist. Weak and pointless, but clenched nonetheless.

He wanted to tell her everything about what he'd seen. About the Heart, about the figure inside the light… about his father. But what would she say? What would Dr. Hughes do?

It'd just be another symptom. Another mark on the chart, and another reason to increase the meds.

So he said nothing.

The monitor beside him beeped again, steady and detached. Counting down or measuring something none of them wanted to name.

Other fragments stirred in his mind—memories still half-formed.

A broken watch, frozen in time… The shimmer of Wild Magic, searing across his vision… And Lirien, her eyes bright with fear and fire.

He locked onto the image of her and held it like a lifeline, even as the rest of him seemed to be slipping away.

Dr. Hughes said something else, but the words blurred out into nonsensical mumblings.

Thane drifted again, sliding between layers of thought, between a world of sterile walls and one of stone and light. One was breaking. The other… unfinished and waiting.

His body sagged deeper into the bed, but the weight in his chest didn't go anywhere. His disease was taking him. Only faster now, it seemed, and he had no idea if she was still alive. If he'd ever see her again.

Thane drifted off and woke later to the sound of nothing.

No footsteps. No voices. No monitors beeping. Just the dim whine of fluorescent bulbs and the whisper of a breathing machine floating through the room like a ghost too bored to haunt.

Night had come. The light through the half-closed blinds was the dull, sodium glow of a parking lot lamp, pulsing gently with wind-cut shadows. The IV stung into his arm and still hung beside him like a stalker that never slept.

He shifted, barely able to move. Everything hurt. Not sharply—just a dull, familiar ache, like his bones had learned how to mourn. His mouth was dry and his throat burned, but he didn't call out. No one would answer, and even if they did, he couldn't care less what they'd have to say.

Slowly, he turned his head. On the bedside table was his father's watch. The crystal face cracked, its hands frozen at 12:21.

He swallowed hard, recalling the henge and the dream-like forest glade where the Heart feed the world, and then he remembered his last glimpse.

12:21… that was the moment Cael stopped the world from breaking… and he broke in its place.

Thane reached out for it, fingers brushing the cracked glass. But it didn't tick, it didn't move. It just sat there, motionless… another thing broken, another reminder of the shadowy voice that had been filling his head with lies.

"Save the Heart." The voice had said.

He scoffed. All lies—lies designed to manipulate and destroy. And Cael had paid the price. So did Arbelon. But it should've been him.

He lay still, the silence heavier than anything he could say or do.

His mind wandered back to the glade. The glow of the Heart and his father's face behind the light. Still and silent.

How was he there? Was any of it real, or was his mind just breaking further?

His eyes closed and Lirien's face rose up behind them. The fear in her voice, her hand in his.

Was she still there? Still safe? Still alive?

He swallowed hard. He didn't have the energy to make sense of it all. All he knew was that he was here, back in the hospital bed. Tethered to machines. Watching the IV pump minutes into his veins while the world he'd left behind bled out.

His hand twitched again, involuntarily. His breath coming thin and wispy, aided by the breathing machine rasping away.

It was all a reminder—he was dying.

That wasn't new, but it was moving faster now. Dr. Hughes had said so. Even his mother knew it—he could hear it in her voice, the way she tried not to let it break. But then the thought came, not fully formed, but sharp enough to catch his attention.

If his father had been there… really there… then maybe…

His eyes dropped back to the watch, its broken face staring back.

What if it's real?

The thought curled around his brain like smoke, too vague to grab, too familiar to shake. Outside, a car rolled past. Headlights flared through the blinds, painting the walls with stripes. Dust rode in the beams like lazy comets. The lights dragged shadows up the wall and let them fall again, like the room was breathing without him.

He didn't sleep again.

He just stared at the watch until the hands on its face started to blur.

The house was quiet. Not the sterile silence of the

hospital, but the kind that echoed—pictures on the walls, light off in every room but his. It smelled like laundry and old memories.

He struggled down the hallway, weak and unsteady, one hand clutched tight around a cane, the other on the wall to steady himself. His legs ached. His balance was garbage. But he made it.

He reached his bedroom, nudged the door open with his cane, and dropped onto the floor by his desk like he was collapsing into a ravine.

The soldering kit was already waiting.

Bits of the headset were laid out across a towel—burned casing, melted wires, screws like dark stars scattered in the fuzz. He plugged in the iron and got to work, hands trembling as he tried to line up filaments no thicker than hair. This was his ritual now. Not recovery. Not acceptance. This. Fixing what was never meant to be fixed.

The iron hissed. He rethreaded a wire. Smoothed a cracked plate. Cleaned a circuit node with alcohol. And then, against every rule of physics and good sense, the logo on the headset flickered blue.

That confirmed it. The headset wasn't broken or dead. It was just damaged, but not beyond repair.

He held his breath. The blue light of the broken circle logo pulsed once, soft and ghostly. He could almost feel it humming in his bones, like the headset was calling to something buried deep inside him.

He reached for it, as if touching it might hold the light steady.

Then sparks flashed and a thin trail of smoke curled from the headset. The blue logo jerked once, twice—then turned red.

A red ring of death lit up like a warning flare.

Thane flinched, instinctively pulling his hands away.

The sharp scent of burnt plastic and silicon wafting in the air. He stared at the headset, heart hammering—not from the pain, but the sudden, brutal certainty: it was broken again. Maybe for good this time.

From behind him, the door creaked open.

"Thane?"

His mom stood in the doorway, backlit by the hallway light, her shadow long across the carpet. She stepped in, eyes on the sparking headset.

"You're still trying to fix that thing?"

He didn't answer. Just stared at it like it had betrayed him.

She crossed the room and knelt beside him, setting down a glass of water.

"It's not going to work, sweetheart."

"It did," he said, voice low. "For a second."

She didn't argue. Just sighed and touched his shoulder.

"They called about the appointment. It's tomorrow morning—early. They want to get you prepped before the injection."

She hesitated.

"They said this is our best chance."

"I know. I was there when Dr. Hughes told us that."

"Thane…" her voice dipped. "Please don't do this."

He nodded, his face softening, but didn't move.

"You should try to get some rest," she said.

She hovered a moment longer, then turned toward the door. "We leave at seven."

Then she was gone.

The door clicked shut behind her, leaving his room with the smell of melted copper and regret. And Thane just stared at the headset, head down, still trying.

He sat cross-legged on the floor, the towel beneath the headset now smudged with burn marks and solder stains.

His hands were shaking. The tips of two fingers were bandaged. But he didn't stop.

He rewired. Slower now. More careful. Like this might be the last time. He fidgeted a few wires in place, snapped a connector in place, and finally, the blue broken circle logo flared to life again.

It wasn't loud, and it didn't flicker like last time. It just glowed, soft and sure. After a few more adjustments, the screen buzzed faintly, then a shimmer of static, and a message appeared, stark white against black:

The Quest of the Heart: Complete

Thank you for playing.

He stared at it. Motionless. The words didn't make sense. That couldn't be it. That couldn't be how it ended.

In the curved glass of the lens, his reflection blinked back—pale skin, sunken eyes, a boy already half-vanished.

His voice came out hollow: "No."

And then—just at the edge of the screen—something rippled. Almost nothing. A shimmer at the corner. As if even now it wanted one last piece of him.

The screen flickered.

Then another word:

Continue?

The font hadn't changed, but the white looked thinner, worn at the edges like paint rubbed by thousands of fingers.

He blinked. Once. Twice. And it was still there, inviting and awkward, like it didn't belong or had slipped through a crack.

Thane leaned in, heart thudding in his chest.

The blue logo flickered faintly.

Then ruptured.

A pulse of static. A crackle of heat. The headset sparked violently, a thread of smoke curling into the air. The blue logo turned red—again—ominous and wrong.

Thane didn't scream. Didn't swear. He just sat there, breathing in the smell of scorched circuits.

Staring at the red circle.

Waiting for it to blink.

But it didn't.

2

———————

HALL OF GHOSTS

The drive ended in silence.

A low whir as the gate retracted. The private transport didn't jolt or rumble—it just glided forward with a smooth electric hum, like it didn't want to wake anyone slumbering inside.

Thane leaned his forehead against the window. It wasn't enough to leave a mark, only enough to feel the cool glass and still pretend it meant something.

Beyond the window a sleek concrete building, three stories of glass and brushed metal, was tucked into a slope of pine and fog. The kind of place that looked like a startup from the outside, but carried the weight of experiments they didn't name out loud.

He glanced over at his mother.

She hadn't said a word since they passed the second checkpoint. She sat upright, arms folded too tightly in her lap, knuckles bone-white. For some reason, she looked smaller today, fragile, like a breath might collapse her.

When the transport glided to a stop, the rear door clicked open with a sterile hiss. Jane stepped out first, her

10

hand clutching the side of the transport, steading herself before lifting her head up and taking in the building that towered in front of them.

Thane followed, slower, his cane clicking on the too smooth pavement. Every movement a negotiation with gravity, every step a contortion. His joints ached. His legs complained. He didn't care about any of this, he knew it was all an elaborate waste of time, but he'd agreed to come to appease his mother one more time.

The air outside smelled like pine needles and ozone.

A security guard stood just inside the main doors—blue uniform, polite eyes, but nothing behind them. He gave Jane a nod of recognition.

She didn't even blink.

Inside, the lights were too soft. The kind of automated glow that adjusted to the movement of bodies and the time of day. Pale blue LEDs ringed the edges of the polished concrete floor, guiding them down a hallway that looked more like a fashion show runway than a medical wing.

The scent shifted. Now lemon cleanser and some kind of sterile lavender. A signature smell. Manufactured comfort.

Muted chimes sounded as the doors opened automatically. People coming and going without a glance in their direction. Heads down buried in tablets, earbuds snugly in place, security badges dangling from lanyards.

Thane walked with his cane tucked close, each step echoing faintly. The place didn't feel like a lab. It felt like a shrine—a cathedral to the dying. He could see it in the polished walls, the curved edges, the quiet hum of machines hidden behind opaque glass.

He didn't speak, but the image rose unbidden—his father here, years ago, striding these same halls with a white coat brushing his knees, nodding quietly to techs who now looked through Thane like he was made of glass.

It wasn't a memory. Or a dream. Just a ghost with a clipboard. And maybe that's all this place was now—a mausoleum with smart lighting.

They passed through another corridor—this one quieter than the others. No chimes. Fewer footsteps, and the hush of recycled air mixed with the distant pulse of machinery.

A few older employees noticed them. Not with curiosity, but with recognition. Awkward nods. Polite, uncertain smiles. One of them, a woman in a white coat with tired eyes, murmured as they passed, "He was brilliant. We still use his models."

Jane gave a tight nod, but her hands twitched. Her fists clenched in that same small way Thane remembered from the funeral. She didn't stop walking. Just moved forward faster.

He watched her closely. There was something brittle in her movements now. Guilt stirred in his gut—not fresh, but familiar. Like rot under floorboards.

At the next junction, the hall widened. A long recessed panel framed in brushed steel sat along the right-hand wall. Within it, a quote was engraved on matte glass in clean, modern san-serif text:

**Every cure begins as fiction.
Our job is to write it into reality.**

The light above the plaque adjusted as they approached—cool white, like spotlighting a piece of artwork or some sacred relic.

Jane stared at it. Her lips parted slightly, but no sound came.

Thane followed her gaze. The words were familiar. His dad used to say them when talking to donors or lecture halls. He remembered hating how confident it sounded. Like his father believed medicine could outsmart the universe. Look at where that got them both.

Footsteps approached behind them—two sets. One slower, deliberate. The other, quicker, lighter.

A voice he knew broke the silence. "Jane, so glad you and Thane decided to come."

Thane turned, just slightly.

Dr. Hughes stood at a respectful distance, hands folded, expression soft. Late fifties, silver at his temples, a subtle hunch to his shoulders that said he'd carried more than a few burdens through life. His coat was unbuttoned, shirt ironed but unassuming. Not trying to impress anyone.

"I know how hard this must be," Dr. Hughes said to Jane, and his voice wasn't just polite—it was personal, different this time.

Jane nodded once, but her mouth remained tight.

Behind Dr. Hughes stood a woman in a slim white coat, glasses reflecting the soft lights. She was clearly younger, straight posture, with a subtle brightness to her that didn't match the building. She looked like someone who smiled easily, even if she wasn't right now.

"I don't know if you remember her," Dr. Hughes said. "But this is Dr. Saito—"

Dr. Saito stepped forward, extending a hand to Jane. "We met at the company Gala a few years ago. It's good to see you again. I'm excited to show you what we've been working on. It all flows from your husband's work. We wouldn't be where we are today without it."

"Of course," Jane took her hand briefly, a smile, the appreciation obvious. "I do remember. It's nice to see you again, Dr. Saito."

Dr. Saito's gaze shifted to Thane, and her face softened —not with pity, but something close to reverence. "Your father… was more than a brilliant researcher. He was a teacher and a mentor. The kind that doesn't just tell you what to do, but makes you believe you can do it."

Thane gave her a guarded look. He wasn't sure what to say. They remembered his father for these things, but Thane only remembered that his disease had stolen him from life too early.

Dr. Hughes stepped in. "We've been working on this for a long time," he said gently, "and this only happens because of you—both of you. Jane made the call. But you… you said yes, Thane."

Jane didn't speak, but Thane could see her blinking hard. Composing herself.

Thane shifted his weight, feeling the fatigue in his joints. His hand trembled slightly as he adjusted it on the cane.

Dr. Hughes noticed. "We've got a room ready just ahead. You can sit down."

"I'm fine," Thane said, reflexively bitter. Dr. Hughe just had that effect on him.

Dr. Saito gestured toward a nearby frosted glass door that brightened slightly as they approached. "This way."

The door to the consultation room sighed open.

Smart glass walls came to life, softly glowing. A curved display already illuminated with drifting neural maps, looping simulation feeds, and strings of code that looked like constellations. Everything was clean and curved—clinical elegance meant to look effortless.

Thane stepped in last, letting the door seal behind him. The chair caught him by the knees before he sat, and he let out a quiet breath.

Dr. Hughes moved to the display. "As I explained at the

house, the treatment involves nanovirions," he began, voice steady. "Programmable, adaptive agents—engineered to detect degenerative neural signals and interrupt their propagation."

He tapped once on the glass. A simulation bloomed—microscopic swarms spiraling around a decaying neuron, flashing gold as they flared against the dying pathways.

"They won't reverse the damage," he continued. "But in the best cases, they can halt the progression. Sometimes they can even reinforce adjacent systems. Create new bridges. New connections."

Thane said nothing. He watched the simulation loop again. His hand trembled faintly in his lap now hidden below the surface of the console.

Dr. Saito stepped forward, her tone gentler. "Your father helped design the original neural interface this all builds on. Without him, none of this would have happened."

Jane stiffened. Just a little. Her hands knotted in her lap.

Thane's voice came low and dry. "If it's so promising, why didn't it save him?"

Silence. A long one.

Dr. Hughes didn't look away. "We were years behind where we are now. He believed in the work. But belief doesn't beat time."

Dr. Saito nodded, quieter. "He was pushing boundaries no one else would touch. This—today—is part of his legacy."

Thane didn't respond. He looked at the glowing diagram again.

Legacy.

That was a new twist, but everything they had tried had a twist, a broken promise. This one would be no different. Another supposed miracle with its own fine print.

Jane stood.

It was too smooth to be abrupt, but something in the motion said *enough*.

"I just need… a moment," she murmured, her voice barely above a whisper. She offered them both a tight smile that didn't reach her eyes, then turned and slipped quietly through the door.

The hush that followed wasn't awkward. Just *heavy*.

Thane didn't look away from the display.

"It's a lot for her," he said, quietly. "First time she's been back here since…"

He didn't finish.

Dr. Saito folded her hands, her tone gentle. "We know. None of us expected it to be easy. Your father meant a great deal to this place. To me."

Dr. Hughes added, quieter than before, "She's doing this for you, Thane. To try and give you a real shot."

Thane watched the neuron simulation on loop—bright flashes of gold spiraling against slow decay. Hope dressed in light and animation, but none of it felt real.

He exhaled, a tired breath through his nose.

"Then let's give her the illusion this might work."

They didn't wait long.

The nurse arrived—young, unreadable, with a professional calm that only cracked when she glanced at Thane's face. Her hands were steady, though. Efficient.

Thane didn't resist as the straps were fastened across his chest and legs. The chair reclined, locking his head in a molded cradle that clicked into place. IV ports hissed. A chill spread through his veins.

Dr. Hughes moved to the interface. "We'll begin with a

low dose for integration. Dr. Saito will handle the pulse sequencing."

Dr. Saito nodded once. "Thane, you might feel some pressure. Vibrations. Some light distortion in your visual field. If it becomes too intense, say something. Otherwise, we'll monitor the response as the nanovirions engage."

Red LEDs blinked to life at the periphery of his vision —slow, rhythmic. Almost like a recording light.

"Three," Saito said softly.

"Two."

"One."

The injection came first, a cold threading through his bloodstream.

Then the pulse hit. It wasn't pain. Not exactly. It was *displacement*. Like sound pressed through bone. A deep resonance behind his eyes, inside his teeth.

The ceiling above him stuttered. Not *flickered—stuttered*. Like a bad video feed buffering. Shapes jerked, lines misaligned, his depth of vision shifted for a heartbeat.

The nurse by the monitor froze mid-motion, syringe hovering an inch above its tray.

And then—

A ring of pale red light. Flickering.

A Graywood Bulwark, towering, half-shadowed, curling in the dark.

A figure suspended in amber light. Unmoving. Faceless. But...*familiar*.

Then everything snapped back.

The nurse completed her motion. The ceiling returned to square. The light above steadied.

Thane blinked hard. His jaw clenched.

No one else reacted.

He lay there, the IV still cold in his arm, eyes on the light overhead.

Had he imagined it?

Or had something looked back?

The light above him dimmed.

Another pulse came—deeper this time, vibrating through his ribs, his spine. His vision pixelated again. A soft static buzzed in his ears like a radio detuning.

And then—

That voice.

Familiar, calm, and unshaken.

"You stayed away. As promised."

Not mocking. Not angry. Almost… *approving.*

Thane tried to move. Nothing obeyed. His limbs, his throat, all frozen.

The voice slid in again, low and even, like it had always been there, just waiting for a quiet moment to come.

"You've proven yourself. Most would've broken. But you… you endure."

The red ring of light returned—this time at the edges of his vision, like an afterimage he couldn't blink away.

Dark fractals bloomed outward from the corners of the room, unreal and pulsing.

"But we don't have to be enemies. You and I—we could rebuild what was lost."

No response formed. But something in him—something hollow and unguarded—*listened.*

"Come back. And this time, it won't be like before. This time, we make it right."

Another flicker.

The ring of pale red light, spinning slowly. A crown of tangled branches, dark and brittle. A glimmering womb of light, warm and pulsing.

And then—

Nothing.

Silence rushed in.

Thane's eyes snapped open, wide.

One thought rose, quiet and uninvited, like a breath he hadn't realized he'd been holding…

Arbelon… it's still there.

Waiting.

And then the light snapped out, and everything dropped into black.

After some time, the light returned in fragments. First the ceiling, then the room. Soft. Too bright.

He blinked hard.

The chair adjusted beneath with a faint whirr, raising him upright inch by inch, like waking the dead. His limbs ached, and his mouth was dry. Behind it, his thoughts felt like someone else's, all jumbled and just out of reach.

And then—

Warmth.

A hand, wrapped around his own.

His mother's.

She sat beside him, her other hand crumpling a tissue in her lap. Her cheeks were damp, but her eyes were dry now, fixed on him with a kind of fragile hope that cut deeper than any pulse or needle.

Thane let out a groan. "Well," he rasped, "that sucked."

Jane laughed. Just once, forced and nervous, like she hadn't meant to.

Dr. Hughes stepped in from the far wall, calm and clinical. "We'll monitor you closely over the next few days. But the early signs suggest stabilization."

Dr. Saito added gently, "We'll know more after the next blood draw, but what we're seeing so far… it's encouraging."

Thane didn't respond. Not really. He nodded, maybe,

or at least didn't object. But in his mind, the words still echoed, soft and serpentine:

Come back.

This time, we make it right.

It hadn't felt like a threat. Something was different about the voice… this time.

He looked at his mother again, snapped back into the treatment room. Her tired face, the wrinkle at her brow she never smoothed out anymore, told her story.

If this bought her hope—even the illusion of it… then fine. He could pretend too.

They left quietly. The halls felt even quieter on the way out. As they passed the wall again, Thane slowed. That quote, etched into glass, glowing faintly.

He stared longer this time. Not just at the words, but at what they might have meant to the man who said them. What they meant now.

And that voice, it still lingered in his mind.

Come back.

He swallowed. Something sharp turned behind his ribs. If his father had really done this—crossed some unseen boundary, reached into *somewhere else*—then maybe this wasn't just medicine. Maybe it was a map. Maybe it was a doorway.

He didn't say a word. Not out loud.

But beneath it, his curiosity bloomed, raw and unformed.

3

SILENCE AND SOLDER

HE'D ALREADY BURNED himself twice.

The soldering iron hissed where it kissed metal, smoke curling up in lazy question marks. Thane didn't flinch. His fingers trembled more frequently now, but he kept working—tweezers in one hand, the singed edge of a power ribbon in the other.

But the headset wasn't cooperating.

The logo that should've glowed soft blue on the front of the unit wasn't just dead. It was worse, it had been replaced. In its place, a dim ring of red light throbbed faintly—taunting him.

He muttered under his breath, dragging the iron in a shaky line.

"Mock me all you want…"

A spark jumped. He hissed and pulled back. Burned again. The third time now.

His hand throbbed, bandaged from yesterday's attempt, and he could still feel the ridged edge of the cracked watch pressing against his wrist. Forever frozen at

12:21. A stark reminder of his failures. His naivety. Of her.

He redoubled his efforts, pushing himself to fix the headset, pushing to fix a world he'd left behind.

In front of him, the headset sat on the desktop like a corpse waiting for autopsy. It was more melted than not—cracked glass, warped plastic, an internal smell that reminded him of charred insulation.

He kept at it anyway. Mostly because there wasn't another choice.

A screw slipped from his fingers and bounced off the desk with a sharp, metallic clatter. He cursed, too tired for volume, and raked both hands through his hair.

Then paused.

Lirien's voice stirred from somewhere deep inside. It wasn't a sound, it was more like an imprint. The memory of light behind her eyes.

"Come back to me."

He stared at the headset. Jaw tight. The red ring snarled again, like it was listening.

"Just keep trying," he said softly, willing himself to press on.

The metallic smell of the soldering iron filled the room again.

He moved slower now, less frantic, more deliberate repetition. Solder. Wipe. Test. Repeat. The occasional flicker of failure buzzed across the rig like a taunt, but he barely reacted anymore. His focus had tunneled. His goal singular.

No schematics. No guides. Just what his dad had shown him, once. Maybe twice. Long ago, but it stuck. The way muscle memory clings to the things you never thought would matter.

A resistor gave way under his tweezers. He nudged it back into place.

His father's voice came back in flickers.

"If the interface resists, you're not speaking its language."

Thane scoffed under his breath, tugging a cable tight.

"Yeah? Then maybe I need to scream."

He sat back in the chair, letting out a deep sigh.

His head turned to the window, eyes gritty, posture stiff with exhaustion. Outside, the neighborhood lay in perfect stillness—hollow suburban silhouettes under a jaundiced moon. Not a single light still on. No movement. No one else up trying to patch together a doorway to a dying world.

Everyone else had moved on. They all had a life to live.

He pressed a palm against the cool glass.

Echo's voice returned—not loud, not present. Just residue. A splinter in his mind.

"You and I, we could rebuild what was lost."

Thane clenched the window frame, jaw tight. He couldn't shake the feeling. Everything about Echo screamed lies, deceit. Manipulation. And now Echo again spoke what Thane wanted most.

He turned from the window, heartbeat dull in his ears. He didn't know what game Echo was playing, but this time he'd play by his own rules—he wasn't done with Arbelon. Not yet.

The console blinked in the dark, and Lirien's voice flickered next. Not a sentence, not even a whisper. It was just a feeling, a presence. Her hand, reaching for him at Skyreach Henge. Her eyes pleading, full of sorrow.

He turned back to the headset. The red ring pulsed. Mocking and smug.

"Come on," he muttered, dragging the power board closer, rechecking the lines. "You worked before."

He adjusted a cable. The glyph flickered—red, then dead again.

He slammed the desk.

The headset rattled. But then it flickered. The blue broken circle sparked to life, soft and faint, but there. It pulsed once. Steady. Alive.

Then it vanished.

Thane slumped in his chair. Bleary-eyed. His hand drifted across the desk and brushed a photo—him and his dad at the lake, sunlight caught behind the peaks.

He stared at it for a long moment.

"How did you get there?" he asked the photo, barely above a breath.

The blue light didn't return.

He stared at the headset for a long while, motionless. Then, head down, he gave it one more try. He slid the casing open again, hands slow and precise now, as if the thing might spook. A quick re-solder to the edge of the damaged feed-line. A breath. A prayer. Then something clicked, and a soft static pop answered.

He froze.

The broken blue circle flared to life, dim but steady. For a moment, it glowed the way it used to—solid, ethereal, like it belonged here.

His heart hammered.

He powered the gaming rig. The old hum returned, both familiar and comforting, but slightly off. The whir carried a warped undertone, just slightly pitched too low, like it was mimicking itself through damaged speakers.

The screen stuttered to life. Fuzz. Then the words, again.

Continue?

It pulsed once. Then glitched—doubling briefly before realigning, steady again.

Thane stared. Then reached for the headset.

No hesitation.

He lowered the headset over his eyes and the words flickered on the screen for a moment too long, then resolved. The screen flashed and cleared with a subtle digital light.

Then something changed.

A pulse, sharp and sudden, ripped through him. Not just in his head, but deeper. Cellular. His body seized with a jolt like static crossing bone. He gasped, gripping the chair arms.

He could feel the movement of his blood, the veins on his arm lit faintly blue, but only for an instant. Then it was gone.

The pressure in his skull twisted sideways. Sound warped, high-pitched tones smeared into bass rumbles. Color stretched, bleeding at the edges of his sight, and then cracked. Fractured lines spidered through the screen. A flash of red cut across the black. Wind roared. Or maybe static. It screamed through him as if sucked through a broken speaker.

And then darkness.

4

BENEATH IT ALL

He didn't wake—he booted.

Darkness, not black, but *corrupted*, like crushed velvet soaked in glitch-static. There was pressure on his chest, on his legs, and his arms. Every breath scraped out like gravel.

Stone surrounded him. Encasing him and pinning him in place.

A hum rose beneath the silence. Not sound, not exactly. More like broken code, scattered and wrong. The kind that vibrated in his bones like a memory that didn't know how to play. Echoes of voices curled through the dirt—*Lirien, Cael, Echo*—half-spoken, half-erased.

Something was trying to remember him. Trying to load him. But it didn't know how, or was uncertain it wanted to.

Then the panic came, sharp and unrelenting. His breath came too shallow. Too quick. His fingers clawed upward, fingernails splitting, his hands scraping stone and packed dirt.

The bitter cold turned to heat. Then the heat to static. Then back again. A loop with no origin and no end.

He choked, but the space around his cheeks pressed in without relief. Dirt filled his mouth with the taste of burnt wire and blood as soon as his lips parted. He turned his head to spit, but there was no space to move, no one to help him.

Then a flicker.

A ring of red light coiled in the dark, just above him, mocking and relentless. It wasn't from Arbelon. It was the *red ring* from the headset, still burned into his retinas. A single blink, like a failed save, then vanished. Leaving behind only the darkness and pressure of the stones.

He growled, tightening his muscles. Then he pushed harder, stretching his hands. His elbows grinding against stone.

Finally, the rocks gave, tumbling away.

His hand broke through first. His fingers were bloody, reaching toward a sky that hadn't loaded for him yet.

Another shove. Purposeful and charged with panic, and finally the cairn cracked open like a rotten egg. A stream of rocks, dirt, and memory spilled out as Thane dragged himself from beneath it all.

From above, the light finally lagged in. Blue sky flickering through black. The distant sky came next, almost like it forgot it was supposed to be there.

He coughed, dirt pouring from his mouth. He rolled out and collapsed on the stone, gasping. The cold air hit last, but when it did, it bit, hard and deep. A wind tore across the henge, rippling banners, but the timing was off. The sound came after the motion, like the world was still buffering, still remembering, and then scrambled to catch up.

Thane blinked hard. The light hit him clean and sharp. Arbelon's sun hung in the sky, but wrong somehow—too bright around the edges. He turned his head away, squinting through dirt-caked lashes.

Then he saw it—*another grave.*

It stood undisturbed beside his own, but stacked with more care. A quarterstaff leaning against it, sun-scorched to a dull gray, worn smooth by wind and time. The sigils that once decorated the wood were half-faded and forgotten.

Thane froze.

His lips parted, but nothing came out.

He knew whose grave that was. Whose quarterstaff lay abandoned. And suddenly the weight returned—not the weight of stone and dirt, but of time and memories.

Everything hurt.

Everything was back.

He stayed kneeling beside the cairns for a moment longer, breath rattling in his throat. The world had finally loaded—the buffering stutter gone—but the light still felt one second too late. Like Arbelon hadn't expected him back.

Then he heard it. Breath, soft and collective, but not his own.

He lifted his eyes.

Figures stood in a wide circle around the twin graves. A dozen at least—some armored, others in tattered robes, heads bowed or faces upturned to the sky. Banners hung loose from spears planted in the stone, their ends fraying, their colors dulled by time.

The moment stretched.

They were looking at him. Not just looking—staring, speechless. They'd seen him claw his way out of his grave. Out of the *stone.* From the *earth.* All in the clear, damning light of day, they'd seen him rise from the dead.

A gasp broke loose—too sharp to be stopped. One

voice. Then another. Whispers rippled outward—shock catching in their throats. A few took a half-step back. One woman stumbled, clutching the arm of the man beside her. Another crossed herself in a shape Thane didn't recognize.

But then amidst it all, three broke from the gathered crowd. Lirien was first. She didn't hesitate. Didn't speak. She just *moved* with a silent regard.

She was across the distance in an instant, dirt scattering beneath her boots, her eyes locked on his. She dropped beside him as he swayed, catching his arm just before his knees buckled again.

Her face was older now. Sharper, but the eyes were the same. Her disbelief rolled into something softer. Relief, maybe, or hope, but it didn't last. Her mouth trembled, just like the others in the crowd.

"Thane, how…" she whispered, her voice catching like the name itself might shatter the moment, fully uncertain if what she was seeing was actually real.

She reached toward his cheek—then stopped. Her hand hovered inches from his skin, trembling.

He didn't pull away. He wanted to reach out, to tell her everything. To apologize about Cael, to apologize for what he'd done to the Heart, but not here. Not with so many other eyes and ears ready to cast judgment.

A sudden motion behind her caught his eye, distracting him. Erynn dropped to her knees beside the cairns. She bowed her head low, whispering something in a tongue that sounded both sacred and broken at the same time. A prayer, or maybe a promise.

One by one, others did the same. Armor creaked, cloaks shifted, and the few Dustwalkers in attendance lowered their heads and murmured a single word…

Celes'tio.

Kaelir didn't kneel or react with the others. He stood

just behind them, his silhouette sharp against the flickering sun. His hand rested on the hilt of his sword, not drawn, but close. Watching. His eyes locked on Thane like a man trying to solve a riddle written in blood.

Around them, the whispers grew, expressions clashed—hope and fear, reverence and dread. Like they couldn't decide whether he was a prophecy fulfilled, or a warning returned.

With Lirien's help, Thane slowly rose to his feet. The rush of breath still felt strange in his chest—like something borrowed, not earned. Every inhale scraped. His ribs ached, and his lungs felt like they were being used by someone else and returned half-cleaned.

He wiped at his mouth with the back of his hand, smearing grit across his cheek. A snarled mixture of dirt and blood. The metallic taste of it all still clung to his tongue.

When he looked up again, the scene bit harder than the wind.

Faces. All around him. Older versions of the people he remembered.

Lirien's hair was longer now, pulled back and streaked with the faintest threads of silver.

And Erynn, she wore armor now, but it didn't suit her. Not because it didn't fit, but because it looked like a wound that hadn't healed right. Dented, scorched, repaired too many times. The girl he remembered was still under there somewhere. But she was buried deep.

Even Kaelir. He had changed most of all. His jaw was sharper. His eyes were harder, as if that were even possible. And whatever had once passed for kindness in his face had been burned away, leaving only iron and edge.

Thane's voice cracked as he forced the words out.

"What... what day is it?"

A beat. Then Kaelir answered, voice clipped: "The Sundering."

Thane frowned, trying to parse it. "The what?"

Lirien straightened, her voice gentle, careful, as if he might break. "A memorial. For Cael's sacrifice. And your… fall to the Echo's deceit."

He blinked. His breath caught.

Erynn's voice was even quieter as she chimed in. "It's been five years…"

She didn't finish the sentence, but she didn't have to.

Thane turned his head, slowly, toward the other grave. The quarterstaff. The sigils. The silence.

"Cael?" he said, though he already knew.

Lirien lowered her eyes and nodded. The truth didn't hit like a hammer. It slid in like poison. Slow, deep, and final.

Five years.

To him, it had only been weeks. maybe less. A fever dream of light and stone and falling magic. But the people around him had aged. Their eyes were heavier, their hope dulled at the edges, and even the wind here felt tired.

The air dragged across his skin like an old memory. He looked down at his hands. Same hands. Same cuts. Same old boots with the scuffed toe. He hadn't changed at all. But to them, he was supposed to be dead. He *was* dead. Buried. Alone. Under stone and time.

And yet—he was here.

He blinked hard, shoving the blur from his eyes, refusing the tears that wanted to come. He remembered it all like it just happened. The henge. The last surge of Wild Magic. Echo's voice twisting through the air like wire. Cael's body falling—slow and final.

He whispered, more to himself than anyone else.

"Cael, he was the hero. Not me."

And still, beneath the weight of it, beneath the guilt and grief and bitterness, something stirred. Hope. If he was here, then maybe it wasn't over. Maybe this was a second chance.

Maybe she could still be saved.

Kaelir didn't move at first. Just stared. Then—one step forward, slow and deliberate. His voice, when it finally came, was too quiet and eerily restrained.

"This could be one of Echo's tricks."

It wasn't said with anger. Not yet. Just suspicion honed to a blade, like he wanted to believe, but couldn't let himself.

Thane turned toward him, eyes narrowed. He was starting to grow tired of this.

"Do I *look* like a trick to you?"

His voice was low. Raw. Every word sandpaper.

He glanced down at himself, at his ragged clothes, half-rotted and stiff with soil. His skin was mottled with bruises, his fingertips still streaked with grave dirt.

"This sure feels real." He ran his tongue across his teeth, wincing. "The dirt in my mouth. The stones. The grave." He gestured toward the cairns, the banners for the Sundering fluttering overhead. His voice caught.

"I was dead," he muttered. "Or at least I was buried."

The words settled like ash, and only a hushed silence followed.

"We buried you together," Erynn said, still kneeling as she lifted her head. Her voice was soft, like a thread trying not to snap. "Because we thought… whatever came next, you'd want to face it together."

A wind moved across the plateau, thin and dry, whistling faintly through the standing stones with the sound of breath lost to time.

Thane closed his eyes. Not to block them out, but

to reach out. Not with hands, but with instinct. Seeking that wild current he used to feel behind the ribs, that second pulse that was never quite his own, that hum had once filled him with the warmth of light through a cracked window. The last time he was on this henge, it had *burned* in him, raw and radiant.

But now? Nothing. No spark. No thread. No fire. Just static. As if the world had forgotten how to render him, and couldn't finish loading who he was.

He pressed deeper, searching past the pain in his limbs, past the rasp in his throat, the ache behind his eyes. And still nothing. Not even silence. Something *worse* than silence —a blank channel, a dead frequency, like tuning into a radio that didn't work.

It all felt wrong in his bones. Before, he had held the key, but it seemed the lock had changed and the magic had shifted. Or maybe *he* had.

He staggered slightly, eyes still closed. His fingers twitched with phantom memory, his muscles trying to remember how power used to flow. But it didn't come.

He exhaled, unsteady. It felt like that broken VR rig back on Earth. The one that sparked, glitched, and died in his lap. Maybe the connection was gone, maybe he broke it, or maybe the world had moved on.

But then, behind his eyes, an afterimage. It wasn't a vision or a hallucination—it was a *memory*.

The womb of the Heart. That golden glow, pulsing with life. It had called to him, once. Filled him with warmth and memory. The hum of old magic and older sorrow. And at the center of it—just for an instant—his father's face. Eyes closed, feeding the world with magical sustenance. Not smiling. Not speaking. Just serene, and purposeful. Then it was all gone as quickly as it had come to him.

Thane opened his eyes.

The henge stones around him shimmered, like a twist in perspective. Edges bending in unnatural ways, and angles folding where angles shouldn't exist. The stone closest to him *quivered*, then snapped back into place as if nothing had happened.

He blinked, and shook his head, but then it got worse.

The people around him—Lirien, Erynn, Kaelir, the others—flickered. Not all at once. Not dramatically. But in *layers*. A man's face dropped into nothing. A woman's outline glitched sideways like a corrupted frame. Then all but the three he remembered most—Lirien, Kaelir, Erynn—vanished.

For a breath, the henge was *empty*.

Then, one by one, the others *repopulated*—like lagged data catching up.

Thane's breath caught in his throat. He staggered again, a tremor running through his knees.

No one reacted. Not a blink. Not a murmur. As if nothing had changed.

But something *had*. Something saw him come back—into the cairn. Something was watching. He was as certain of it as he'd ever been about anything.

He turned slightly to Lirien, voice barely a whisper.

"Something saw me. Or is watching us…"

Lirien looked up. "What?"

He shook his head, eyes scanning the stones again. He turned toward the quarterstaff at Cael's grave. The banners above still fluttered—but somehow, even they seemed out of sync.

"We shouldn't stay here long…"

A silence stretched between them.

Erynn rose slowly from where she'd knelt, brushing grit

from her knees. The look on her face wasn't awe anymore. It was urgency… and fear.

"There are things you don't know," she said, her voice steadier now.

Kaelir stepped forward, interrupting. "We still don't know if this is all real, if that's really Thane. Doesn't this all seem too convenient?"

"Stop," Erynn snapped at her brother. "This is a sign. You'll see soon enough. For now, just hold your venom for the forces of Devendor."

She paused, turning back to Thane with a breath and a hushed voice—polished now, confident. "There are things we've learned. And I just know you've come back for a reason. But if we're going to survive what's coming…" She paused, her eyes turned north, toward the hazy outline of distant mountains, and her voice dropped to a whisper. "… we need to head south, to Felderwin. Fast."

Kaelir shifted. His hand moved from his sword hilt, his expression didn't soften, but he didn't argue either.

Lirien knelt briefly by her pack and pulled out a folded gray cloak—worn, but clean. She stood and offered it to Thane with both hands.

For a moment, he didn't move. The wind picked up, sharper now and colder. It bit through the sweat on his skin and raised gooseflesh along his arms. He started to shake his head out of pride, maybe, or habit, but then he met her eyes and took it with a nod.

The wind moved again, tugging at the wind-worn banners above them, and Thane looked out across the henge one last time. Its stones jutted at odd angles, and some were cracked and fallen. A reminder of the damage done in his last visit to this place.

This was the place where everything had ended. And now it was where it would all start again.

Thane stood quietly, the cloak swaying in the wind, his fingers twitching in the cold. He didn't feel reborn. He felt dug up. Pulled from the earth like a relic nobody asked for.

Around him, the gathered mourners had gone quiet. Some stared like they'd witnessed a miracle. Others—like they'd seen a mistake, but the murmurs had mostly stopped as they watched the exchange between Thane and the others.

"Enough," Kaelir snapped, voice taut with command. "We don't have time to gape at ghosts."

Someone inhaled like they wanted to argue, but Kaelir silenced it with a look.

"You heard him, if the Riders are tracking us, we'll never outrun them on open ground. We split. You all make noise, draw them off toward the way we came. But move fast."

He turned to Thane, Lirien, and Erynn. "You three—come with me. We'll take the Broken Path."

It wasn't a request.

The crowd stirred, moving to comply. Armor buckled as farewells were murmured. Horses shifted under the weight of unspoken fear. There were whispers of prophecy. Of resurrection. Of hidden signs.

But Thane didn't hear them. He was staring at the cairns. Kneeling down, he laid his hand on the stones above Cael. Cold spread through his fingers, and a sudden grief pressed behind his ribs. That memory was *real*—not a glitch, not a dream. That was what made this worse. Because of what he'd done, Cael was really gone.

He was still staring when a hand brushed his wrist.

It was Lirien. Her fingers rested there for just a second —warm and certain—before slipping away again without a word. He looked up to say something, anything, but her back was already turned, moving toward Kaelir, toward the mountains to the south of them.

Whatever this was—whatever had brought him back or allowed him to come back—it wasn't rest, and it wasn't for fun.

It was to fix things, to help these people.

It was the road ahead.

And he followed.

5

AND HE FOLLOWED

THE TRAIL HAD no name in the maps of Arbelon. But Kaelir called it the *Broken Path*.

It lived up to it.

There was no road—just a thread of churned dirt and shattered stone that cut through the lower ridges of the Skyreach Mountains. A route once used by shepherds and smugglers in older, quieter times. It rose and fell like a drunkard's gait, hugging slopes that tried to shake them loose, winding through canyons narrow enough to trap a breath. The mountains pressed close on either side, and every step felt earned in bone.

Thane's legs burned. His chest felt hollow. Sweat clung to him like another skin, and his boots sucked at the grit like they meant to stay behind.

But it wasn't just the terrain. There was something about the silence here—too deep, too wide. Like the mountains themselves were holding their breath. Even the birds had abandoned them. Or maybe they just knew better.

Kaelir moved at a brutal pace. Lirien followed in his

wake, her hood drawn, eyes on the ground. She hadn't spoken since they left the cairns behind.

Erynn, though, was still Erynn in the ways that mattered. Still a fount of knowledge.

"Devendor didn't fall in battle," she said quietly, as they rounded a bend that looked down into a barren gulch. Her voice had a distant edge, like she wasn't sure if she believed what she was saying. "It… folded. That's the word the survivors used."

Thane glanced at her, waiting for more.

She kept her eyes forward. "They said there were whispers in the mountains. Voices that weren't theirs. People waking up screaming without knowing why. Then the Riders of the Ring started hunting their own."

She finally looked at him.

"Some swore Echo spoke from their fires."

That stopped him. Not the meaning, but the image. A fire, crackling. Friends around it. Warmth. And then a voice from the coals, from the smoke, from the flickering dark—

Not just watching.

Speaking.

Kaelir didn't turn. He just said, flatly, "It serves him now. All Devendor's resources falling in line to a common end."

They kept walking.

There was no comfort in their movement—only necessity. The slope steepened, forcing them to grab at gnarled roots and exposed rock. Somewhere below, a loose stone clattered into nothing.

Thane caught Lirien watching him, just for a moment.

Then her gaze broke, and the silence deepened.

Whatever Devendor had been before—the thought of it now in the grip of Echo—it meant more darkness ahead.

The world was changing under their feet. And with every mile, Arbelon felt less like a dream and more like a ruin waiting to remember it had fallen.

They climbed in silence, the air thinner now, steep walls to either side. The trail curved sharply, then flattened just long enough to offer a view.

Kaelir raised a hand, and the group stopped.

Before them, the ridge-line split to reveal a sweeping valley far below, golden with dead grass and fractured by old stone fences—the remnants of some forgotten farmland.

And it was there that they saw them. The main party. Half a dozen or so figures, cloaked and hunched, winding slowly along a narrow cut that led south toward lowlands north of Felderwin.

For a moment, Thane felt something like relief. They'd made it that far. But then, a shape tore across the horizon, rising up from the fields of golden grass.

A rider cloaked in black and sharp-edged, astride a grey mount—lean and taut—moving faster than it had any right to. Then another followed. Then three. And then more, too many to count. They broke like a swarm of hornets from the western edge of the grasslands, moving as one. Like they'd been *waiting*.

The Riders of the Ring.

As the first one reached the road, steel flashed in the sunlight. One of the cloaked figures below fell to the ground, hard and motionless. The others scattered, barely time to scream, but the horses screamed for them, maddened by the sudden onslaught.

Thane's breath caught, a spike of helpless fury rising in his throat as he stepped forward. Kaelir's arm a bar against his chest, eyes warning him to stay put.

Then there was a shriek, shrill and deep.

The sky cracked.

Wings, wide and leathery, swept down from the ridge high above. Two drakes, grey as ash, each with a rider in drab leather armor, reins in one hand and a long pike in the other. They closed in on the scene instantly. One struck from the air, slamming into the nearest Rider of the Ring mid-gallop, tearing the man from the saddle and tossing him aside like a stray toy.

The other drake dove, loosing a howl that split the valley like a blade.

The Riders turned, spurring their horses—fleeing in all directions without a plan, only survival. The drakes screeched again, setting off in pursuit.

Lingering behind the evolving chase, the survivors of the main party scrambled into cover. One burly figure heaved the fallen man over his shoulder, limping after the others.

"Veilborn," Erynn whispered.

Kaelir nodded. "I'd heard rumors that they were flying again."

Thane stared.

Not because he understood it. But because of the way fluid and coordinated manner in which the drakes moved. No wasted motion. They weren't wild things. They were smart, intentional.

Kaelir's jaw flexed, unreadable.

"We move," he said finally. "Now."

He didn't look back to see if they followed.

They moved again, faster now. Kaelir's stride was long and deliberate, driving them into an even tighter switchback on the far side of the ridge. The cries in the valley faded behind them, swallowed by stone and distance.

No one spoke for a while, but the silence had changed.

It wasn't just caution now. It was tension, wound tight between them like thread stretched too far.

Thane found himself next to Lirien at one point, but she didn't acknowledge him. Her hood stayed low, shadowing her face, and when he slowed a step to catch her eye, she didn't return the glance. Not exactly. She just looked through him, and what he saw there chilled him more than the wind. There was hurt. Buried, but real.

She hadn't spoken to him since the cairn. Not even a nod. In the past, she wouldn't hesitate to flare at him, and that's what bothered him the most. If Lirien went quiet, then the cuts must be deep—deeper than even the hurt he delivered upon her already.

He didn't know what to say. Everything that came to him since pulling himself out from under the rocks, he dismissed. So her pressed on, and instead, he looked down at his hands. They didn't feel like his. Callused from climbing, scraped, dirt-caked. They felt like they belonged to someone else, like they just weren't his. And his watch— sweat pooled beneath it on his wrist, and it was still screaming 12:21 at him. Reminding him when the world stopped, or at least changed last time.

The wind picked up, dry and full of weight. They climbed higher still, the trail nothing now but broken shale.

Out of nowhere, Erynn appeared beside him, bright-eyed and curious.

"Were you anyway? On Earth?" she asked, voice low but eager.

He blinked at her. "What?"

"Don't act like it's not strange. I mean, you did seem to die here. But you didn't, did you?"

Her tone wasn't challenging. Just hungry for understanding, or for confirmation that some of the impossible things she believed might be true after all.

He hesitated, uncertain if he should answer, but then it hit him. Cael was gone and if there was anyone here who was going to be able to help figure out what the hell is going on, it was her.

His shoulders relaxed. "Yes. I was on Earth, but things…" he paused. "Things there are getting worse… for me, especially."

"But you look the same, like a day hasn't passed for you. How is that?" she asked.

"I don't know. Things—a lot of things—are different this time. I thought I might come back to find everything just as I left it, like the other times. But this? This is crazy," he said, searching for some more clarity, some understanding of what all had happened in his absence.

She leaned in, her voice low. "Don't let them get you all wound up. We're all happy to have you back, not to mention the Wild Magic."

Thane stared at the ground ahead without a word. Every step grated against his spine, and his breath came shallow. He didn't know what was going on with his magic, but he wasn't about to volunteer anything just yet. Not until he knew more. A lot more.

"It hasn't been easy for me," he said finally. "Being away. After what I did. The last thing I remember was seeing Cael fall, and Lirien…" His voice trailed off, and he turned away, wiping a tear from his eye. He gathered himself, turning back, "And then everything went black, and I was gone. Everything was broken, including me."

He could feel the IV from the hospital in his arm, the antiseptic smell as if here were back there. His stomach turned.

"I'm not dreaming," he added, more to hear himself say it aloud than for any other reason. "This place is real."

Erynn fell quiet beside him.

Up ahead, Kaelir glanced back. Just once. Then he turned away and kept moving. Relentless.

They climbed for another hour before the path flattened into a rare stretch of open ledge, just wide enough for them to catch their breath. The sun, if it still hung above them, was hidden behind stone and haze. Time felt like it was fraying at the edges.

Thane paused, resting a hand against the cool rock wall. Something in the air… changed.

A stillness bled in. Subtle at first, then total. No breeze. No grit. No sound. Even the ache in his legs quieted. The others didn't seem to notice, or if they did, no one spoke.

Then sparks flashed subtly, bleeding in, faint, like static in his peripheral vision. Flickers of blue-white light danced in the corners of his eyes and vanished when he turned his head. The scent of burning plastic tickled the back of his throat—sharp, synthetic, and wrong.

Thane flinched and staggered. He grabbed at the wall, steadying himself. Whatever it was, it wasn't pain. It was tuning, like a signal searching through static, slowly clicking through empty channels until it found him.

And then he felt it. *Not* a voice. A *presence.*

But it wasn't loud or sharp, it was just there. A low vibration, almost thoughtful. As if something immense had simply leaned closer.

"Haven't you always wondered why you could do what others couldn't?"

The words came—not into his ears, but directly into his mind.

"Why you could touch the Wild Magic? Why it listens to you? I gave you that. As I gave you life."

Thane's breath hitched. The presence wasn't invading. It was listening.

"Get out of my head," Thane growled under his breath. The words came out harsher than he expected.

There was a pause, then a quiet laugh. It wasn't cruel or gloating, just familiar. Almost… fond.

"We're more alike than you know, my son."

The words crawled under his skin.

My son.

He froze. The words hit him square in the chest, unwelcome and impossible, but something deeper than logic trembled in him. He shoved it down, focused on the heat in his veins, on the rough stone beneath his palm. And for a moment, he felt it recede. But it didn't vanish or break. It just retreated.

The stillness broke like a snapped string. The wind returned, whistling along the cliff face, and someone coughed behind him. Erynn mumbled something about water.

Thane blinked.

The sparks were gone. So was the scent. But something in him had changed. He didn't know how—only that it was *his* push that sent Echo away. He'd *closed a door*. And now, for the first time, he wondered if another had been opened.

They didn't make it far, maybe twenty minutes before twilight pooled between the peaks, thinning the air and blurring the world into a violet haze. The wind came harder now, pulling at their cloaks and stinging their eyes. The group moved in a loose line along a narrow rise, hugging the wall to their right when Kaelir stopped cold.

His hand shot up.

"Hold."

Thane's nerves bristled. At first, he heard nothing, only the scrape of stone under boots, the wind rasping past his ears.

Then it changed.

The wind bent.

There was a shape behind them on the ridge trail, some fifty feet back, slumped and limping.

Lirien stiffened as Kaelir reached for his blade.

The shape staggered forward, head low, moving with an unnatural rhythm, like its limbs only half-remembered how to bend.

Then Thane saw it. Not the face. Not at first. But the shoulders. The slope of them. The twist in the gait. The cloak—torn on one side, just like—

Thane froze.

He couldn't breathe.

"Cael…" he whispered.

Erynn gasped, but Lirien's voice was the one that broke first.

"No," she said, hoarse and low. "That's not him."

The figure jerked to a stop. Its head snapped up, eyes like dying coals burned in the sockets—faint red, not alive, not rage… just *wrong*.

The thing flickered—*twice*. A rendering glitch. A ghost caught between frames.

Then it spoke.

"It's all right, Thane… you did what you had to… just like he wanted you to."

Each word broken and glitched as if spat from a corrupted drive. Audio distortion over cracked memories.

Thane stumbled backward. His hands sparked, but nothing came. No heat. No magic. His body remembered something, but his mind didn't.

The thing stepped closer.

Kaelir didn't wait. He moved like a drawn bowstring, forward in a blur, blade flashing silver in the last light of day.

The creature hissed, but it was too slow and too broken.

Kaelir struck once. Then again.

The revenant dropped. It didn't scream. It didn't cry out. It only whispered, through broken teeth and twitching lips.

"Father… sees you now…"

Then stillness.

Kaelir stood over it, panting, a dark red streak on his blade. His shoulders heaved once, and then he wiped the sword on his cloak and walked away. He didn't say a word.

Everyone stood frozen for a moment looking at the fallen form, but Kaelir moved away, and finally, they all turned and followed. Not because they wanted to, but because *not* moving meant thinking about what they'd just seen. What it had said.

Father sees you now.

Thane didn't want to know what that meant.

The trail narrowed again, carving a jagged route down a hillside that overlooked the lowlands beyond. The mountains fell away slowly, opening into a wide basin of fog and ragged pine. Somewhere out there Felderwin waited, but the world between here and there felt foul and distant.

The crumbled stone beneath their feet shivered and slid just enough to make rocks clatter from the path and vanish into the mist below. It wasn't an earthquake. It was something smaller and more personal.

Thane stepped forward and the tree beside him flickered. Just for a blink. A tall pine. There. Then *not*. Then back again. He stopped, heart thumping, and reached out to touch the tree, just to confirm it was real.

No one else seemed to notice. Or maybe they just didn't want to.

A few steps later, he watched a rock blink out beneath

Kaelir's foot, and then return just as the heel lifted. It was like the world was buffering, struggling to load its own assets.

Thane's hand twitched at his side. The Wild Magic stirred in him, but it felt brittle, like a wire frayed from within. He reached for it and sparks trickled across his knuckles, sharp and blue, but *off*. Like a dying console gasping on its final boot.

He bit down a curse.

Kaelir glanced back. His jaw was tight, and his voice tighter.

"We need to get to Felderwin. Now. There's no more time for rest."

No one argued.

The ground ahead cracked slightly under their steps. Not loud or deep, but enough to remind them that Arbelon wasn't just breaking metaphorically anymore. It was breaking *for real*, and every step toward Felderwin felt more like a race against collapse.

The mist thickened as the mountains gave way. Their path dipped into a valley, low and wide, ringed by broken ridge-lines and pockets of forest that looked scorched at the edges. Somewhere in the fog ahead, the ground flattened, and the first signs of civilization emerged.

The Capital City of Felderwin did not glitter. It just *loomed*.

At first, it was just outlines in the haze. Then the gloom of morning light—grey and dour—caught it.

Crowned by its upper keep, the city's castle was carved straight into the bone of a jagged bluff that raised high above the horizon. The city itself spilled downward across terraced slopes, its crooked rooftops rising in uneven tiers. Stone towers jutted like ribs through its layers, some intact, some crumbling, their tops flattened by age or war. Massive outer walls circled the lower city—scarred and cracked, but still standing.

Beyond the walls, a wide bog spread in every direction —a tactical floodplain ringed with trap mechanisms and sluice-gates. Raised wooden walkways, warped with rot and time, zigzagged across it like the remnants of a shattered web. Some sunken halfway, others still intact.

"They can flood the whole basin if they have to," Erynn murmured, stepping up beside Thane. "It's built to be siege-proof."

Thane said nothing. His eyes traced the sluggish river cutting through the heart of the city, water brooding under the fleeting morning haze.

Felderwin wasn't just a city. It was a statement, but it was barely holding together, mostly by habit it seemed. They reached the edge of the bog, where a single narrow boardwalk arced across the waters.

Kaelir stepped onto it first. "Stay close. Don't stop."

The wood groaned under their feet, wet and unsteady. Water sloshed beneath, thick with silt and shadow. Somewhere out in the fog, something large stirred—once, then again, vanishing beneath the surface with barely a ripple.

No one spoke. The silence wasn't reverent. It was *watchful*. Each step careful, with purpose.

Halfway across, Thane slowed just enough to glance back. The highlands were gone behind the mist. Only Felderwin remained ahead, the great city wall rising like a scar across the horizon, jagged and pitted, but *defiant*. The outer towers showed signs of battle. Black scorch marks, shattered arrow slots, and a collapsed turret on the western flank, but no breach.

The city had survived. Barely.

As they neared the far side of the walkway, a bell rang

once—dull and mechanical—from somewhere inside the wall, but no gates opened.

The group paused on the stone landing just shy of the entrance, cold water dripping from their cloaks and armor. Above them, sentries peered down through misted slits, their forms barely visible. Banners, burned and tattered, hung limp beside the parapets.

The wind shifted and somewhere in the city beyond, another bell rang. This time deeper and slower. Then a reply came, and then silence again.

Thane glanced up.

The crest above the gates had nearly eroded with time, but enough of it remained to make out the ancient symbol —a sun, cleaved in two. Half gold. Half black.

He shivered. Not from the cold, but from the feeling that the sun itself might never rise here again.

6

THE DEAD DO NOT KNOCK

Two LARGE BRAZIERS flanked the city gates, blazing in the dreary morning air, smoke rising in a dirty plume marking the stones of the city wall above them with a black soot. From a small window above the city gates, a torch flared to life, and a voice barked out.

"Stop where you are!"

Erynn stepped forward, her eyes upward to the guard. She raised her forearm, taking a small piece of iron the shape and size of a matchstick that hung from a chain around her neck, and pressed it to her skin. A moment later, a rusty red spiral spun to life on her arm, glowing with a magical light.

"I hear at Lady Aelith's command. We bring news from the north."

The face disappeared, the torch with it. Seconds stretched into minutes, as Kaelir paced back and forth, growing more impatient by the minute.

Thane pulled his cloak tighter. The fabric was still damp from the crossing. Mud clung to his boots, flaking in dry chunks.

"What is taking so long?" Kaelir asked, pausing by Erynn, his eyes hard. "See. This is why I don't come to the city. These times demand—"

His voice was cut off by the sound of the outer gates creaking open, but they didn't open all the way—just enough for a single line to pass through. A narrow crack yawning between timeworn iron, hinges grinding like a breath dragged through rust.

From inside, the city exhaled.

Just beyond the narrow gate, the road funneled toward a wide causeway. Guard posts flanked either side with makeshift shacks attached to a formal gatehouse, lamps burning low behind slatted shutters. No banners flew. No bells sounded.

Figures emerged from the gloom—five guards, rough-armored and tight-shouldered, weapons sheathed but hands hovering near the hilts. None looked older than thirty. All of them looked afraid.

Thane stopped without thinking. The others followed suit—Erynn a half-step ahead, Lirien drifting closer to his side than she had the day before.

The lead guard approached slowly. His eyes scanned the group, lingering on Kaelir's weapon, on the grime crusted across Thane's sleeves.

"Travelers don't come to Felderwin in the early morning hours anymore," he said, voice flat but tight. "Not unless they're running from something."

Kaelir crossed his arms. "We're not travelers. We're returning."

The guard tilted his head, unconvinced. Then his eyes narrowed.

"What's your name?" he asked, staring at Thane.

Thane met his gaze without blinking. "I doubt it would help."

The guard frowned. "Try me."

A pause. Then: "Thane."

Nothing happened.

The guard's mouth opened, but whatever name he'd expected, whatever reaction he'd braced for, it wasn't that one. His eyes flicked to the others.

"He died," someone muttered from behind the line. Another guard, just loud enough to be heard.

"Five years back," said a third. "At Skyreach."

Erynn stepped forward. "He came back. I said we had news from the north for Aelith. Now let us pass." Her voice was firm, commanding.

But the guard didn't move. The torch in his hand flickered once, casting Thane's face in quick flashes—sunken cheeks, dirt-streaked brow, a long, pink scar fading down his jaw.

The lead guard looked him over, jaw tense. "Could be a trick," he said quietly. "There's Wild Magic out there now. Echo plays games with faces."

Lirien's voice cut through the fog. "And if it is a trick, Aelith will know. Let her decide."

The guard didn't respond right away. He stared a moment longer, long enough to make Thane feel like a memory being measured against a rumor.

Then he lowered the torch. "Escort them to the Inner Ring. I'll send word to the Steward's Hall."

Someone grumbled behind him. The youngest of the guards, maybe. "If you are who they say you are," he muttered, "then you shouldn't be here."

Thane almost smiled at that, but he didn't.

Two guards waved them forward as Erynn led the way, the guards falling in silently behind them. The streets beyond were hushed and wet, the flagstones slick with morning mist and lined with the brittle edges of frost.

Smoke drifted from low rooftops, thin and sour, curling against the sky like something trying to escape.

Felderwin did not feel like a capital.

They walked a winding path through the city's lower tier, where stone buildings gave way to stacked shanties and rain-slick oiled skins. Boarded-up shopfronts bore words scorched and half-peeled. A shattered archway sagged inward where a tower had once stood. Across it, a canvas banner hung crooked—painted hastily in black:

Only Believers Can Hold the Line.

They passed a baker's stall with no bread. A wellspring fountain, bone dry. On the steps of a broken chapel, a woman sat rocking a child who didn't move.

Thane said nothing, but his fingers twitched.

They passed a courtyard with a statue at its center—a noble figure carved from greenstone, now cracked straight through the heart, headless. The First King of Arbelon. As if the defacing could be any worse, someone had thrown red paint across it, and the color bled like a wound.

Thane stopped, pausing just long enough for the cold to settle in his bones.

"What happened?"

Lirien's voice came low beside him, eyes never leaving the path ahead.

"Veydris fell. Devendor closed its gates. The north was lost."

She hesitated—just for a breath. Then continued.

"Then they came for Felderwin. When Chancellor Verrick died in the siege, every House in the city tried to claim the mantle. But none could hold it. Aelith stepped forward—not because she wanted to, but because she was the only one left with both a sword and a voice worth listening to."

Kaelir, who'd been silent to this point, finally spoke. His voice was gravelly and distant. "Even when they gave her the nod, they only called her a Steward. They meant it as an insult. But Stewards don't seek crowns, they just hold the line while the rest of the world falls."

The road curved again, rising slightly toward the Inner Ring. Watchtowers loomed above them—old stone layered with new wood, the repairs obvious and ugly. Thane could feel the city watching from shuttered windows and dark corners. No one waved. No one welcomed.

They passed a small cluster of tents near an alley, refugees maybe—tattered clothes, blank stares, a child tracing runes in the mud with a twig. Echoes of the rot Devendor brought to the world.

Thane glanced back at the defaced statue.

"Feels like the city's held together with ghosts and glue."

Lirien didn't argue, and the others remained silent.

Ahead, another castle wall rose from the earth. The Inner Ring.

As they approached, a different set of guards, older than the last, their armor cleaner but their eyes even wearier. No one spoke as they moved through tighter streets and narrow alleys. The air was colder here. Quieter.

The Steward's Hall stood at the edge of a long court-yard, its arches scarred by fire, its banners faded to ash-grey. A carved relief above the entrance showed the same symbol from the city gates—a sun, cleaved in two. Half gold. Half black.

Inside, the reception chamber was dim, lit only by a few hanging lanterns and the pale light that leaked through high, narrow windows. The ceiling hung low. The room felt confining. Dust clung to the edges of the short desk, its surface hidden by piles of scrolls, stacks of books, and behind it stood a closed door.

Sitting on the corner of the desk was a single figure. An aging man with thin, sharp-features, his robe lined in red and frayed at the sleeves. He clutched an ornate brass-handled cane in one hand, the other rested on his lap. His eyes were rheumy, but there was nothing soft in them.

"What is this news you bring," he said without introduction.

"We will only share that directly with Aelith," Kaelir muttered, coming to a halt in front of him.

The man ignored him. His gaze moved to Thane, and stayed there.

"You're him," he said. "Or the one claiming to be."

Thane stepped forward. "You don't believe me?"

"I don't believe in ghosts," the man said flatly. "And I don't mistake tricks for miracles."

"He's not a trick," Erynn said, stepping forward.

"Then prove it," he said. "Show me the magic. If he truly is who you say, then it should answer to him freely."

Thane's jaw tightened, about to speak, but Erynn cut in before he could. "Aelith trusts me with her mark. But you know that already, don't you?"

The man stood from the desk, cane clicking on the ground to help him. "It is not that Erynn, you are young. Age brings a certain clarity... certain caution that this city needs desperately."

"Damn it, Ryndel," Kaelir said, his voice flaring. "We finally bring something to Aelith... something that—"

Erynn interrupted. "Something that can finally bring some hope back to this desperate fight. I assure you, Ryndel, this is Thane. He is back."

Ryndel turned away, his cane clicked the floor as he paced, deep in thought. Finally, he turned back, his eyes studying Thane for a moment too long before he shook his head, turning back to Erynn.

"You know as well as anyone—Wild Magic can mimic appearance. And memory. The Echo can twist both."

Erynn stepped forward, her voice firm. "You think I don't know that? After everything we've been through?"

Kaelir pushed his way past Erynn, glaring at Ryndel. "Enough of this. We're wasting time. We're here to see Aelith."

"And Aelith will see you when she's ready. But I don't take chances with strangers who might wear old faces like masks."

Thane opened his mouth, but Ryndel cut him off with a raised hand.

"The dead don't walk back into council halls, Thane. Not on my watch."

Silence settled like dust.

Then, just as the tension spiked, footsteps echoed from behind the door and it creaked open.

Aelith entered first. Not dressed in finery, but wrapped in a long gray cloak hemmed with red stitching, marked with the red spiral sigil of Veydris. Her hair was tied back in a simple braid held by the same pin of ambered glass, what had been pale wisps of faded starlight years ago, now streaks of white cutting through dark strands. Lines carved her face deeper than Thane remembered. Not old, just *worn*, and her eyes didn't shine, they measured, carrying the weight of decisions she never asked to make.

Behind her came Vesha.

Her armor was dented and charred, pauldrons misaligned, chest-plate bearing a deep scrape across the crest of her House. Her head was half-shaved now, the other side matted and tucked behind one ear. Her eyes still held the rust-haze of the Wayfen, a fresh scar running along her collarbone. She said nothing, but her presence was reassuring, especially after what they'd seen in the grasslands below the henge.

The room shifted. The weight of command had entered. Even Ryndel stepped back without protest, bowing slightly as he returned to his seat behind the desk. The others fell silent.

Aelith surveyed the group in one slow pass. Her eyes paused on Kaelir, then Erynn. Then finally on Thane.

A beat of silence stretched. She studied him like a memory trying to reassemble itself.

Thane didn't flinch, but he felt it—her eyes weren't looking at him. They looked through him, into the cracks he hadn't bothered to hide.

She stepped closer.

"I've visited your burial site," she said at last, her voice quiet, without ceremony.

She paced a slow arc before him, eyes searching for something just beyond reach.

"And now here you are… but there's something different in you."

Thane didn't look away. In fact, he'd felt the same thing himself.

Behind her, Vesha's voice cut the air like a knife. "Something *missing*."

Thane's jaw ticked. He met Aelith's eyes.

"I didn't come back for reunions."

The words landed harder than intended, perhaps misplaced in this chamber, but spoken true.

Another silence. Not shock, just heavy.

Aelith blinked once, then glanced past him toward the gardens in the courtyard outside the chamber.

"No. The time doesn't permit us such luxuries, does it?" she said in agreement, turning back to Thane.

Aelith's words still lingered in the air, but it was Vesha who broke the silence.

"How did you come back?"

There was no hostility in her voice, just the same low, unsettling suspicion Thane had seen mirrored in every wary glance since Skyreach. In every question he didn't answer.

Aelith watched him carefully as she spoke. "We doubted the words that came from the gate. That you were here. But I see you now, the same as you were five years ago when you first visited Veydris. Still, no one has explained how a dead man walks."

Thane's eyes narrowed slightly. "Does it matter?"

"Of course it matters," Vesha said, stepping forward, the edge in her voice sharper now. "Not just to us. To the city. To the war. If we put faith in something false—"

"She's right," Aelith said, quiet but firm. "We must understand what brought you back."

Thane hesitated. The words were there, he just didn't want to say them. Not here. Not yet. His silence stretched a breath too long.

It was Lirien who finally spoke.

"He didn't come back alone."

All eyes turned to her. She looked pale but steady.

"It wasn't just him that crawled from the cairns," she continued. "There was… something else."

"What?" Aelith asked.

Lirien glanced at Kaelir, then Erynn, before saying the name.

"Cael."

Ryndel made a strangled sound in his throat. Vesha blinked once. Then again. Aelith froze.

"Cael is dead," said Ryndel, voice brittle. "He's been dead for five years."

"I know," Lirien said. "But he followed us. Until…"

"Until I dispatched the thing for good," Kaelir added, his voice cold.

There was a long pause.

Vesha's hand drifted near the hilt of her blade, her eyes connecting with Kaelir's. "A revenant?"

Lirien didn't answer. Kaelir simply nodded.

"Then how do we know *you're* not just another puppet?" Vesha said sharply, turning her gaze back on Thane. "A soul stitched together with magic. A face molded by Echo's will."

It hit hard, and Thane, already strung tight, snapped. His voice was cold and cutting.

"I died for this world. And it buried me."

He stepped forward, meeting Vesha's eyes directly.

"So don't ask me *what* I am now."

Silence. Again. But not the kind that waits for answers. The kind that *doubts* them.

Aelith exhaled, slow and shallow.

"Settle, Vesha. We're running out of time to question *how or why* the world brought him back to us. This is a time for action, and however uncomfortable it may be, we must place our trust in this moment."

No one moved, but the doubt didn't vanish. It simply held its breath and slipped into the shadows.

Aelith turned, the faintest edge of weariness crossing her face.

"We can spare you temporary quarters in the East

Wing. You are to remain within the Inner Ring under our protection until I've had time to assess this situation."

It was diplomatic, but not a request.

Kaelir bristled. "We don't need your protection. That's not why we came here."

Before Aelith could reply, Erynn stepped forward, her voice calm but firm.

"We don't have time to waste. And you know it."

Aelith raised an eyebrow.

"The Athenaeum," Erynn said. "We need access to the archives."

Ryndel scoffed behind her. "You think books will win this war?"

Erynn didn't blink. "No. But answers might."

Aelith studied her for a long moment. Her gaze shifted to Thane, then Kaelir, then back to Erynn.

"Rumors of the Chosen One are already whispered. If I let you go wandering Felderwin, I lose more than I gain —especially if half the city believes he's truly returned. You know what they will think."

"They're not wrong," Lirien said. "And why hide it? Announce his return, let it be known. A little hope can go a long way."

"And we don't need to wander," Erynn said quietly. "We'll stay in the stacks, out of sight, out of earshot. You can manage the message here, but allow us to not waste what little time we have left."

Silence again, then Vesha let out a breath and finally nodded. "I hate to admit it, but it's a decent plan… under the circumstances."

She didn't sound happy about it, but she didn't argue either.

Aelith gave the faintest nod in return. "Fine. Go

straight to the Athenaeum. No detours. No conversations. Once you're there, stay put until we send for you."

Her eyes settled once more on Thane.

"But know this. Your purpose here is clouded to me. So I am trusting you to be honest to your words. And if you break that trust… no one in this city will bury you a second time."

She turned and left without another word. Vesha lingered a moment longer, her gaze unreadable, then she turned and followed.

Only once the door clicked shut did anyone breathe, but the silence thickened.

Ryndel didn't speak. He simply returned to his work, muttering something inaudible as he flipped open a ledger.

A page entered from a side alcove, arms folded with a small bundle of neatly folded clothes—clean, simple garb in muted grays and blacks, the fabric worn but mended. He offered them to Thane without a word, then exited just as quietly.

Thane turned from the others, stripping his dirty burial clothes off, replacing them with the new ones. The clothes smelled fresh and clean, but did nothing to wipe the dirt and grime from his skin.

Lirien stood nearby, arms crossed, gaze distant. She hadn't said a word since Aelith left. Her stance was casual, but there was tension in the set of her shoulders.

Thane finally spoke, voice low and rough, just loud enough for Lirien to hear.

"They think I'm one of Echo's toys."

Lirien's eyes flicked toward him, then settled.

"Then show them you're not," she whispered.

The words landed with an intentional force, bereft of any hesitation.

Thane looked down at his hands, flexing his fingers as if unsure they still belonged to him. Then he turned slightly, catching his visage in the window's warped reflection—barely a silhouette in the gray morning light.

"If I still can," he muttered, even softer than before.

Neither of them spoke after that, but the silence between them felt less distant now.

7

FORGOTTEN WORDS

THE TABLE LOOKED like it had survived a storm—books unstacked, parchment curled at the edges, a scatter of half-spilled ink. In the center of it all, hunched and unmoving, sat Erynn. Her fingers gripped the worn Codex in her lap, knuckles white against the spine cracked with age. The margins were filled with faded notations, the lines of text curling at odd angles, symbols inked in a looping hand Thane didn't recognize.

But Erynn did. It was her mother's handwriting, a litany of clues and clarifications. She flipped back a page. Then forward. Then back again. Her lips moved in a whisper, not quite sane, but not quite madness either. Her fingers traced along with handwritten words on the page.

"Fall of the Heart… echoes through the stone… wrong archive…"

The rest of the group stood in an awkward semicircle around her, unsure whether to speak or wait. Scrolls had been laid out next to maps, which laid by half-translated sketches and rubbings. But she ignored them all, focusing only on the Codex, and something she clearly couldn't see in it.

Thane watched her thumb through brittle parchment like someone searching for a ghost. Her hair had come loose from its braid, falling across her cheek as she leaned closer into the pages, eyes scanning with frantic rhythm.

Lirien finally broke the silence. Her voice was quiet, careful.

"Erynn… what are we even looking for?"

No answer.

The lantern light flickered. Somewhere in the distant levels of the Athenaeum, a bell tolled softly measuring time that didn't matter here.

"She wouldn't have written it unless it mattered," Erynn muttered at last, not looking up. "Not in the Codex… it's in her own hand."

Kaelir shifted behind her, arms folded tight. His voice was flat. "Our mother wasn't all there in her final days. We both know that."

Erynn's spine straightened. Her gaze didn't lift, but her tone sharpened.

"Careful."

The warning cut sharper than steel.

A silence followed. Longer this time. Even Kaelir looked away.

Thane crossed his arms, watching them both. The air in the room had thickened, like it did before a storm. Only Erynn kept moving.

"There's something here," she said quietly. "Something she marked years ago. She believed it was hidden in Felderwin. But the note doesn't say where. I can't even tell what exactly I'm looking for."

Her fingers trembled slightly as she turned another page. It crackled like dry leaves.

"But it's here. Somewhere. I know it."

She stopped, just for a moment. Her voice lowered.

"I wish Cael were here."

The words struck the room like a dropped stone. Everyone looked at Thane, but he didn't say a word. He stayed motionless, his eyes fixed on the Codex in Erynn's lap, like it might swallow them all if it wanted to. Then Erynn's head snapped up, her eyes flashing with sudden clarity.

"The documents from Salile, the ones recovered just after the Rending. They were never catalogued in the upper halls."

Lirien blinked. "So?"

"They would've been sealed…" Her breath hitched. "In the lower archives."

She stood up so fast her chair skidded back across the floor, and she grabbed the lantern.

"Come on. We're wasting time."

Kaelir frowned. "Erynn—"

But she was already moving, Codex hugged to her chest, steps swift and sure.

"To the lower archives," she said. "The old ones. We'll find it there. I'm certain of it."

The others hesitated a moment longer, but then followed.

The stairs wound down like something half-forgotten, carved into the stone before the Athenaeum had walls, before Felderwin was even a name. Dust clung to the lantern light as they descended, a slow spiral deeper and deeper through levels untouched by recent memory.

The air cooled with each step. What began as the dry archive-scent of paper, ink, aged wood, gave way to something older. Mineral and roots, like breathing through the bones of the world.

Erynn led without speaking, the Codex cradled at her side. The fire in her eyes hadn't dimmed. If anything, it had grown sharper, more focused, now less of the desperation, replaced with inevitability. She knew where she was going, even if she didn't know what she'd find.

The others hustled to keep close. Thane brought up the rear, hand trailing lightly against the stone railing. It was cold, slightly damp. His fingertips tingled where they touched it.

The stairs ended and a passage opened into another level, this one even stranger. The archive alcoves that pockmarked the hall held no shelves, only small crystal tubes lined the walls and in each the discolored edge of parchment. Scrolls packed away like frozen memories. As they moved forward, halls forked and twisted through what looked like the roots of ancient trees, petrified in place. There were more crystal tubes, more scrolls, but ahead the faint flickering lights played across curved walls decorated with murals that seemed to animate when glanced at from the corner of the eye, freezing the moment anyone looked directly.

Lirien paused, staring up at the image of a woman cloaked in flame, arms outstretched to a city crumbling into ash.

"Did anyone else see that move?" she whispered.

Kaelir didn't answer, but Thane caught the way his hand drifted toward his sword. Just in case.

The whispering started not long after. Not voices exactly, more like the echo of thoughts and memories threading through dust. Faint and unintelligible, but there.

They descended a short flight of steps to another landing, and that's when Thane saw it—carved into the stone beside the arch—a weather-worn sigil, twining branches encircling a single flame.

He froze mid-step.

"I've seen that before," he muttered.

The lines of the symbol shimmered faintly, then glitched. For half a second, the branches twisted and became something else entirely, but then blinked back into place. Lirien didn't notice. She had already turned down the next passage, but Thane lingered a breath longer, staring at the mark.

It was the same symbol from the faded banners inside that sanctum near Trosten. The one that offered hope and hospice from the Riders so long ago. The one Cael had shared with them.

These lower levels weren't just an archive. This was an Alumata Sanctum.

He moved again, not certain if this place brought ruin or riches. His experience with the sanctums had been mixed at best, the last in the Great Forest being a place of rot and lies. He didn't know what to trust, and that same doubt Aelith had shown him—he felt it now, mirrored in himself.

They reached the end of a hall that opened not into a room but into the side of a cliff. A wooden bridge, narrow, ancient, and slick with condensation, spanned the gap across a vast underground cavern. On either side, sheer rock walls vanished into shadow above and below. Somewhere far beneath them, water flowed.

The sound of it rose in the silence. A distant, steady current. Not rushing, not still, but steady and constant. The bridge creaked underfoot as they crossed. Far below, torches flickered in a perfect ring, outlining a small dock that jutted into the dark. Thane could barely make it out, the distance too great, and vertigo gripped him.

He swayed.

A sudden lurch toward the edge—

Lirien's hand caught his arm, steadying him. Their eyes met, a silent moment passing between them, but neither said a word, yet everything understood. She pressed on as Thane gathered himself. His breath fogged in the cold, sharp as iron in his lungs. His skin prickled. He couldn't tell if it was the chill, or something deeper rising from below. But whatever it was, it was unsettling.

Erynn reached the far side and stopped before a smooth, seamless vault set deep into the wall. The door was circular, etched faintly with runes too worn to read, but no lock or handle was visible.

Lirien stepped up beside her.

They studied the door in silence, fingers brushing its smooth surface, searching for something unseen, something forgotten. But the stone didn't move as they found no crack or split in the wall. Nothing to open it.

And yet, something shifted.

A ripple passed across the surface like light bending through water. Dust lifted on a breeze that hadn't been there a moment ago. The runes glowed faintly, then faded again.

Behind them a voice, low and layered, emerged from the silence.

"Even voices have weight. And you've brought more than one."

The group turned sharply.

Thane hadn't heard a step. Not a sound. But there, standing in the passage behind them, was a figure draped in robes the color of aged wood and moss. His body looked as if it had been shaped from vine and bark, each limb interwoven like the roots of a living tree. Where skin should have been, there were ridges of grain and glistening resin, and even from this distance, Thane caught the scent of pine. One of the creatures eyes was milky, clouded with age. The other, sharp and bright, gleaming with a green so vivid it seemed impossible this far underground.

The creature bowed his head slightly, as if greeting old acquaintances.

Lirien inhaled sharply, but Erynn stepped closer.

"Thassriel, Alumata of the Ninth Grove," she whispered. "You do us a great honor with your presence."

Kaelir blinked. "He's real?"

Thassriel tilted his head.

"I have not had any visitors in some time. Since your mother's passing."

His voice was like layered wind, echoing as though it passed through trees before reaching the ear.

Thane didn't kneel, but he did step back as Thassriel approached the sealed door. There was no gesture or incantation, only a simple word.

"Open."

The wall responded like breath exhaled. Runes lit faintly, then dissolved, and then the stone receded without cracking, folding inward like mist pulled into a single point. Beyond it, a chamber waited, but Thassriel didn't enter, he just stepped aside as the others slowly filed inside.

The chamber was round and low-ceilinged. Dust floated in golden shafts of lantern light, catching on ancient records that lined shelves along one of the walls, and opposite it parchment scrolls rested in recessed slots. Runes were etched into the stone itself—spirals of glyphs encircling the scroll nodes like nerves wrapping bone. Scattered Codex fragments lined a raised central table—scraps of vellum covered in half-legible annotations. The smell was old parchment, burned oil, and something metallic underneath.

On the far wall opposite the doorway, a patchwork of sketches were pinned up with rusted nails protected within frames of lattice-cut wood. Most were of Arbelonian land-marks—mountains, valleys, temples long since buried or consumed, but one sketch stopped Thane cold. It was a valley, wide and sunlit. Framed by cliffs with jagged ridges rising behind it like broken teeth. A waterfall spilled from one side, and in the clearing below gentle trees bent in the wind.

It looked like Salile. It *should* have been Salile. But he knew it wasn't. The angle. The grain of the cliff face. The way the light fell across it. He'd seen this place before. Walked there as a boy.

Yosemite.

He moved toward it slowly, almost unwilling. The parchment had yellowed with age, the ink faded to near sepia. In the bottom corner of the sketch there were three letters scratched in a hand he would know anywhere.

T. A. A.

Thomas Alexander Ash—his father.

Thane's stomach dropped. He didn't speak a word. He couldn't move, but he didn't let his eyes linger too long either. Inside, his thoughts spun. The letters were in the same hand. It was the same valley. It could only mean one thing. The same impossible truth that had haunted him since Skyreach.

His father had been here. He had drawn this, and had somehow stood in both worlds—Earth and Arbelon.

Thane stood silent, taking it in, parsing his thoughts. Thassriel stepped to his side, his voice hushed as the others dove in to the mystery of the archives.

"Your gaze lingers in old light. Is it known to you?"

Thane turned to him, not certain how to answer, but he was saved as Erynn called out from the table across the chamber.

"Thassriel, please. I need your help locating something my mother wrote about years ago."

They turned, moving closer.

Erynn leaned over the table, turning over one of the etched diagrams. "These are… tied to the Codex. Some of these phrases… they match my mother's notes."

Thassriel nodded slowly, eyes drifting across the chamber as if cataloguing the room not by sight, but by memory. As he approached the table, Erynn laid her mother's Codex down, opening it and pointing to her handwritten notes.

The Alumata's expression was unreadable, his ancient features carved with patience. He gestured to a nearby wall that was etched with lines of script.

"Someone long ago arrived at our shores, back before the Rending. He carried strange knowledge, and dying breath."

Thassriel's voice was quiet now, almost reverent.

"He gave his life. And in return, Arbelon was given time."

Kaelir stepped closer to the table, brow furrowed. "The Heart?"

Thane felt unmoored.

Thassriel didn't answer, not directly. Instead, he traced a hand over a slab of ancient stone, one that held a broken stanza that was barely readable.

"The Heart will break when one calls it by name."

Thane's gaze flicked to the words, and then back to the sketch, but he said nothing.

The silence in the room stretched as they all tried to work out the riddle of the etched words. Then, almost absently, Thassriel's gaze dropped to the watch on Thane's wrist. He stared at it for a long moment as a recognition flickered in his eye.

"Where did you come by that trinket?" he asked.

Thane didn't answer right away, and his voice felt stuck in his throat.

"It was my father's."

Thassriel nodded once, and in that single motion, both gentle and knowing, Thane understood. The truth he'd buried was deeper than he thought, and it had roots in Arbelon.

Thassriel's gaze lingered on the watch a moment longer. Then, without lifting his eyes.

"May I?"

Thane hesitated, his fingers curled around the band at his wrist. Even now, after everything, it felt like the one thing still tethered to his life before, to his life outside this place. But slowly, he unfastened the clasp and placed the watch into Thassriel's waiting hand.

The Alumata's fingers moved with care—root-wrapped digits gently turning the object over like it might fracture under breath alone. His bark-skinned thumbs pressed a hidden seam on the backplate with practiced ease.

A faint click. Then another, and the inner mechanisms opened with a shiver of ancient metal. What lay inside didn't look like any gear work Thane had seen before. What should have been brass was streaked with something darker, veins of faint blue etched through the steel like living circuitry. And buried at its core was a glimmering coil, pulsing softly.

Thassriel whispered in an older tongue, words that slipped between breath and rustle, as if spoken through leaves. He shifted something with the tip of a fingertip and a spark flared, brief and violet, then gone.

The watch ticked to life. Off-beat and erratic, like a heartbeat trying to remember how to beat. But Thane immediately felt it, a warmth at the base of his skull. It wasn't pain, it was something stranger, like memory pressing inward or a thought that wasn't his, forming only halfway.

Thassriel's voice barely rose above the whisper of the room.

"It was damaged when the Wild Magic took hold. But not lost."

Another adjustment. Another flicker inside the casing.

"Its purpose has changed now." He looked up, meeting Thane's eyes. "Like yours."

Thane tensed. The words landed like prophecy or judgment. He wanted to look away, but couldn't. Thassriel closed the backplate and turned the watch over once more. Then, with both hands, he returned it to Thane. The moment it touched his skin, it pulsed once, warm and alive, in recognition. Thane flinched.

"How did you fix it?"

Thassriel stepped back, his gaze unfocused—as though listening to something deeper than the silence.

"It is what I do. But please know that it no longer amplifies what is within," he said. "It now listens. Mends that which is in need. Giving life."

Thane looked down at the watch. The faintest glow stirred beneath the faceplate, subtle and almost imperceptible.

A long moment passed.

The faint pulse of the watch faded beneath Thane's sleeve. Whatever warmth it held, it cooled quickly like it had given all it could, for now.

No one spoke. Even Erynn, still hunched over the Codex, seemed momentarily lost in thought. Then she looked up.

"So, what are we supposed to do with all of this?" Her voice wasn't frustrated exactly, just tired and frayed.

"I don't know what this means. How do we fix the Heart?"

Thassriel didn't respond immediately, but when he did, his eyes drifted not to her, but to Thane.

"The Heart is not a wound to be healed. Not by any who did not shape it."

He turned from the table, one hand brushing gently along a stone wall etched with looping diagrams—designs half-familiar, half-alien. His fingertips traced them like he was reading something old and personal.

"You seek to mend a thing you do not yet understand."

He paused again.

Then he tapped a particular carving near the top. It looked like an archway or maybe a rift.

"Yes, there it is. There are still those who might remember how."

He stepped back, voice low but sure.

"Go to the village of Swain. It lies at the edge of what once was. A place warped by forgotten magic. A crossing, long sealed, but now undone."

His tone changed slightly, sharper now, though still soft.

"Beyond the Veil lies Faelenshara. The Fae once stood beside the Architects. If any remember how the Heart was shaped… it is them."

Erynn stepped closer. "The Fae? They've been gone for—"

"Not gone," Thassriel interrupted. "Withdrawn. Waiting." His gaze darkened. "But beware. Echo walks freely now, and not all who pass through the Veil return."

The words had barely left Thassriel's lips when the sound came. A low rumble, distant but deep, like the world itself had groaned in warning.

Dust sifted down from the arches above. A lantern near the far wall guttered once… then blinked out. Several shelves trembled, and a scroll slipped from its cradle and slapped to the floor. Another followed. Then a sconce snapped loose, metal clanging as it tumbled across the floor, spilling flame across the rug that spanned the room.

Erynn jumped back. Kaelir drew steel. Thane and Lirien froze, but Thassriel didn't flinch. He moved to action, working to suppress the fire before it spread.

Then from behind, footsteps echoed. Fast and approaching.

They turned just as Vesha skidded into view at the edge of the doorway. Her braid was half-loose, eyes wild but focused.

"Aelith sent me. Felderwin is under siege," she said, breath short but steady.

Another tremor rippled through the stone above them, but closer this time. Dust leapt from the stone like sparks.

"I need to get you out," Vesha continued. "The river below. It's the only way, but we have to move. Now."

Another rumble rolled through the foundation. A bookcase creaked, then collapsed completely, crushing half the scroll table and scattering its contents across the chamber. The fire on the rug was spreading.

Erynn hesitated. "But we need to help—"

"Go," Thassriel said firmly, moving to the flames with bare hands. "I will manage this, but you should not linger. Knowledge casts long shadows."

His robes fanned smoke as he turned to the fire, already chanting low words in a language Thane didn't know. His silhouette blurred behind the rising haze—half-plant, half-memory.

Thane clenched his jaw. One last look at the sketch on the far wall. The watch pulsed once on his wrist.

Then he turned and followed the others. Vesha leading the way.

8

THE WATERS BELOW

THE STAIRWELL CURLED DOWNWARD like a stone throat, wet and dark and narrowing with every step. The further they descended beneath the archive, the more the air thickened—damp, metallic, and ancient. But it wasn't rot, just the memory of things that had once rotted, long ago.

Torchlight sputtered, catching on sweat-slick walls and iron sconces bent with rust. Shadows slipped sideways along the stone. Thane kept his hand against the wall to stay upright, his legs turning to rubber from the sheer number of steps they were descending.

Vesha led the way, torch in one hand, dagger in the other, with Kaelir right behind her, sword still drawn. Erynn followed, eyes flitting across each shadow like they were counting teeth in the dark. Lirien stayed close to Thane's side, her silence steadying.

They reached the bottom with a hush. No voices, only footsteps and the sound of water lapping somewhere beyond. The passage opened into a cavern. It was simple. No grand archways or glowing glyphs, just a collapsed dock slouched against a half-sunken wreck.

Thane stared at the boat, but it wasn't a boat. It was a corpse. It sat moored in the black water like it had always been there, its hull split open and furred in pale mold, the deck warped and drowning. A thick moss crawled up the half-collapsed mast, choking the insignia carved into the wood. Inside the hull, water shifted like breath in a dying lung.

Erynn stepped forward, brushing a layer of lichen from the gunwale. Beneath the smear of age, words emerged in an old script, barely readable in the low light.

"This is it," she whispered. "The *Keshari Braid*. It never left the tunnels. They waited for the waters to fall… but they never did."

Kaelir spat without looking. "It's a ghost ship."

Thane glanced toward him, eyebrows low. "You believe in ghosts?"

"What do you think you are?"

Thane shrugged his shoulders. "Funny," he chuckled.

Vesha moved closer to the edge, crouching near a rusted winch embedded in the dock stone. She ran her hand across a chain the width of her wrist, the iron links groaning with age and extended out above the river, attached to the ceiling—rusty hooks dangling from it at regular intervals.

"This place was primarily for trade," she murmured. "The whole network ran off the Andriel tributary. Back before the Rending, you could sail the waterways all the way from Devendor in the north to the oceans in the distant south."

"Doesn't look very sail-worthy," Thane muttered.

"It wasn't meant to sail," she said. "At least not under the city. The Chainpull system moved these boats by those rigged hooks hanging from the chains in the ceiling of these caverns. They'd winch forward one link at a time, dragging them through tunnels."

She stood, wiping her hand clean on her cloak. "But the river tunnels collapsed, and the water flooded in. The boats in here couldn't go forward, couldn't turn back. So they stayed. And rotted."

Thane stared at the wreck again. This place didn't feel like an escape route. It felt like a crypt.

Another low boom echoed from above, and dust rained down.

Thane looked up. The iron hooks dangled from the ceiling swayed ever so slightly in the stale air. The track they hung from disappeared into blackness, winding deeper through the caverns like some forgotten spine. Some hooks were crusted with rust and half-submerged in blackish water. Others, closer to the dock, hung free and sharp, as if still waiting for orders. Still, the tunnel ahead narrowed. There was no clearance for boats, and no light beyond the flicker of the torches. The air pressed tighter around them. It reeked of old water and iron, like blood trapped beneath stone.

Vesha knelt beside a half-rotted crate tucked behind a collapsed supply barrel. She pried it open with the blade of her dagger, wood cracking like bone. Inside were four leather masks. Each one fitted with a rounded glassy stone at its center—veined in faint, flickering blue.

She held one up.

"Breathstones," she said. "One breath gets you about two minutes. That's it. Then you resurface or drown… eventually."

Thane frowned. "That's it? That's the escape plan?"

There was an uncomfortable pause. Vehsa's eyes were on him, steely and unwavering.

"Unless you have a better one?"

Lirien cut the tension, stepping forward, taking her mask, though her jaw clenched as she turned it over. The leather was slick with age, the inside stained dark from years of wear. She pressed it to her face, and the stone let out a soft, vibrating hum. Her eyes fluttered briefly, then steadied. After a moment, she shuddered and pulled it off.

"It feels like it's breathing for you," she muttered.

Erynn raised hers and sniffed the leather. "It smells… musty."

Kaelir didn't comment. He just checked the strap, tugged it tight, and hooked it onto his belt. Ready.

As Vesha passed the last mask to Thane, his watch flickered. Just once. A quick stutter of light beneath the face, then gone before he could focus. He blinked, shook his wrist, but nothing happened. He turned the mask over in his hands. The leather felt clammy in his grip. The stone inside was cold—colder than it should be.

Thane looked down the tunnel again. A thin fog slithered above the water's surface where the ceiling dipped so low the hooks and chain disappeared. He held the mask in his hands, swallowing hard. The fog curled tighter. Something brushed the edge of Thane's boot, barely more than a ripple, but it was enough.

He stepped back, startled, nearly bumping into Lirien.

"What?" she asked, her voice low and agitated.

He glanced down. The water had gone still again, undisturbed, but something in his chest had turned cold. Then he felt it. It wasn't in the water, it was on his wrist. His watch was glowing. Not red or flashing, just subtly warm and alive. He lifted it slowly. The crystal face didn't flicker this time. It held a steady glow, a soft light behind the face, like it was backlit by something internal. But it wasn't showing time anymore, it was showing something else.

"What is it?" Erynn asked, noticing the glow.

Thane didn't answer. The heat from the watch wasn't hot exactly, but it pressed into his skin with purpose. But not like before, when it flashed wildly helping him hold his magic in check. No, this was different. This felt more deliberate. Steady. Like a heartbeat that wasn't his.

He glanced back toward the tunnel—and froze.

Ripples moved on the water. Not waves. Just small, concentric rings from somewhere deep in the dark, a single disturbance, spreading outward. All without any sound or splashing. The ripples had already faded, swallowed by the murk, but Thane couldn't shake the feeling pressing down on him. The glow of his watch. The Breathstones. The ghost ship. The tunnels narrowing ahead.

This wasn't just an old trade route. It was a way in. A backdoor. And something had already used it.

He swallowed. "We're not alone."

Everyone went still.

The silence after Thane's warning stretched too long.

Kaelir raised his sword. Vesha gripped her dagger. Lirien stepped closer to Thane, her gaze fixed on the water. Even Erynn stopped breathing.

Then came a sound, barely audible, like wet cloth being peeled from stone. From the black water beyond the dock, three shapes began to rise.

Slowly. Too slowly.

Their heads surfaced first, wrapped in soaked linen, bandages stitched with threadbare symbols that glowed faintly as they met the torchlight. Their faces had no eyes and no mouths, only the shape of a head bound in layers, the cloth seeping like it was still bleeding.

Next came their torsos—bare and carved with deep scars, the wounds deliberate, ritualistic, intersecting in spirals across their chests and bellies. The cuts glistened, not with fresh blood, but with something darker. Oily and ink-like. In one hand they held a bone-saw machete, its teeth jagged and blade too long. In the other, a forearm shield, its surface rippled with algae and streaked with quartz-colored slime.

Their movement was slow but synchronized. They rose not with splashes, but with dripping silence, as if the water itself recoiled from them. When they finally stood at full height in the shallows, the three Gutter Saints moved in perfect unison. Heads tilted as one. Weapons lifted—not to attack, but to mark Thane.

And then, they spoke.

One voice, shared between three mouths. Dry and crackling, like parchment being torn.

"The Chosen returns to walk among the unclean. We've been sent to bring you home. If you follow, the others will be spared."

Their machetes stayed at their sides, and they didn't advance. They waited.

Lirien stiffened beside Thane. Vesha muttered a curse under her breath. Kaelir held his position by Vesha, ready to intercept.

The only one to move was Thane.

His watch still glowed faintly on his wrist. He raised it slowly, keeping his eyes on the intruders.

"Last time this lit up," he growled, "I nearly destroyed the world."

The glow pulsed, soft but steady. A heartbeat. He took one confident step forward, his eyes glaring.

"Walk away while you still can."

The Gutter Saints did not speak. They simply stepped forward all in pace, in eerie synchronization, blades lifted, heads tilted slightly, calling his bluff. They were not afraid. They'd been sent to collect him.

Kaelir didn't wait, the second the Saints stepped forward, he struck, blade flashing in torchlight as he surged past Thane and met the first figure head-on. The clash rang out like steel on an iron bell. Sparks jumped and water exploded from the impact, spraying across the dock.

Kaelir pressed the attack with brutal force, each strike hammering into the Saint's shield, then blade, then shield again. But the Saint didn't falter. He absorbed the blows with that same eerie stillness, like each parry had been rehearsed a thousand times before.

Their blades locked at the edge of the water, feet skimming wet stone. Kaelir snarled. The Saint didn't even breathe.

The second Saint moved in parallel—gliding, not rushing—toward Lirien and Erynn. Without a word, they split to flank him.

Lirien's weapon hissed to life in a shimmer of white-blue light, her pommel unfurling into a luminous blade. She didn't wait for Erynn—she lunged. The Saint countered with a wide sweep of his machete, the serrated edge missing her neck by inches.

Erynn dove in low, catching the Saint's leg with a sweeping kick that unbalanced him just enough. Lirien brought her blade across his chest—sparking against his shield.

He didn't stagger. He pivoted, swinging hard. Erynn ducked, blocked with her forearm, and winced as the crack of bone was unmistakable. Yet, she still moved, and still struck back.

The third Saint raised his machete and started toward Thane, but Vesha moved faster. She slipped between them, both daggers drawn, a hiss escaping her lips as she launched herself toward the Saint's midsection. The blades hit, one glancing off the shield, the other slicing along his ribs, but the Saint didn't flinch. His counterblow sent her sprawling backward across the stone with a curse.

The Saints fanned out, each one matched to a defender—every motion clean, exact, ritualistic. They didn't grunt or scream, and they didn't speak. They fought like monks giving communion, like priests offering blood.

The clang of steel rang out like a hymn twisted into violence. Each strike, each block, echoed in the cavern, loud and final.

Lirien was bleeding now too—cut deep across her thigh. Erynn dodged a follow-up blow rolling hard on to her damaged arm, face twisting in pain, but she rose quickly. Together they closed in, Lirien drawing the Saint's attention while Erynn circled to flank.

Kaelir shouted and feinted low. His opponent moved to parry, but Kaelir twisted, brought his blade up in a brutal arc, and drove it straight through the Saint's throat. The blade punched out the back of the Saint's neck. Steam hissed from the wound.

Still silent, the Saint collapsed.

Across the cavern, Lirien ducked a wide swing and drove her blade upward beneath her Saint's ribs just as Erynn caught the arm at the wrist and twisted, holding the shield away.

The second Saint twitched and shuddered. Then fell still.

Only one remained.

And he was already turning back toward Thane, slow and inevitable, as if he'd never been concerned with the others at all. His machete raised defiantly, his eyeless face fixed on Thane.

Vesha didn't hesitate. She rose to her knees and sprang forward, daggers flashing. Her footing was clean, her stance low—every movement sharp and deadly. She feinted left, then dove right, driving one blade toward the Saint's exposed ribs.

But this time, he was ready.

The Saint pivoted with unnatural speed and brought his forearm shield across with a sickening crunch. It caught Vesha mid-turn, her ribs cracking under the blow, before the machete came down in a brutal arc across her side. The sound was wet and final.

Vesha dropped.

She hit the dock hard, one knee catching the stone before she collapsed fully, her body twisting as blood spilled beneath her. Her hand gripped her side, but the wound was already soaking through—too wide, too deep.

"Vesha!" Kaelir shouted, but he'd never have reached her in time.

Thane acted before he thought. Pure emotion. Pure venom. The glow on his watch pulsed and then flared. It was different this time. Hotter. Brighter. It didn't shimmer or flicker like before—it *burned*, white and pulsing, like something inside it had cracked open.

His rage broke free. He stepped forward, voice ragged, the sound tearing from his throat like something being ripped loose.

"You're fucking dead!"

The air around him quivered. But the air didn't just quiver—it tore. A pulse radiated from Thane's body like a silent shockwave. There was no wind or sound, just pressure rippling through water, stone, and bone. His feet left the ground. Only slightly, but enough. Enough to feel the air slip beneath him like silk caught in fire.

The cavern responded.

Moss erupted from the stone in every direction unfurling like time reversed. Thick green tendrils curled across the dock, the walls, even the ceiling. Hooks overhead rusted backward—gleaming as if new. Cracks in the floor sealed shut. The dock groaned as wood fibers stitched themselves whole. And out in the black water, the *Keshari Braid* shuddered… and began to mend.

Splintered ribs of its hull curved inward. Mold peeled away like shed skin. Ropes reformed. A lantern blinked to life, swinging lazily from the bow.

Life was returning, but not just to the ship. A soft light crawled across Vesha's broken form. The flow of her blood slowed. Then reversed. Thread-thin filaments of glowing gold webbed out from her wound, crawling beneath her skin. Her breath hitched, then steadied. The wound sealed before their eyes.

Across the cavern, Erynn gasped and dropped to a knee as her arm twisted unnaturally then popped back into place. The bone had reset. She flexed her fingers. No pain.

Lirien stared at a jagged slash across her thigh and watched it vanish beneath fresh skin.

No one spoke. Eyes wide.

Kaelir turned just in time to see the third Saint—the one who had dropped Vesha—looming behind her, machete raised, ready to strike again. Without a word, Kaelir hurled a dagger across the chamber. It struck the Saint squarely in the forehead. The linen split. The blade buried to the hilt.

The Saint dropped with a thud, but then behind him, the other two were stirring.

The first Saint—the one Kaelir had killed—twitched. A sound like wet cloth peeling from bone echoed through the chamber. His hand flexed. His head jerked to the side. Steam hissed from his neck—not fading, but coalescing. *Reknitting.* Skin began to close.

The second Saint—felled by Erynn and Lirien—was rising again, also mended by the magic.

Thane didn't move. His body was locked in rage, glowing wildly, like the magic was using *him* now, not the other way around. It was rewriting the room. Blindly, beautifully… terribly.

One Saint took a single step toward Thane, but he never made it further. Vesha's hand shot out, gripping the Saint's fallen machete. She moved before anyone could react.

One smooth motion, up onto her knees, spinning with the blade in hand. Her wound should have kept her down. Her ribs should have shattered her breath. But the Wild Magic had mended more than bone. It had rearmed her. She rose in a fluid arc—spinning low, then striking high. The bone-saw machete screamed through the air and took the Saint's head clean off.

The linen didn't tear. It *burst*, and steam hissed as the body slumped backward into a heap.

She didn't stop. Pivoting hard, Vesha drove forward on instinct alone, her bare feet sliding on slick moss as she launched herself at the second Saint, the one now halfway risen. This time, no spin. Just pure rage. She planted one foot, brought the blade around and cleaved straight through the Saint's neck with a brutal, final chop.

The head rolled. The body collapsed sideways, twisting unnaturally, limbs twitching once before falling still.

Vesha stood above the remains, chest heaving, her eyes lit with fury—and something brighter. Magic still clung to her skin like static. Her wounds had healed, but the rage remained.

And then Thane screamed. His voice cracked wide, raw and filled with something too big for sound. Light exploded from him. It didn't flare. It *erupted.* His spine arched, arms thrown wide. His feet left the ground again, but higher this time. Fully airborne, suspended by something unseen. White-gold light poured from his mouth, from his eyes, from the tips of his fingers.

It bled into the air. No spell. No incantation. Just raw, screaming power.

Everyone turned just as the blast hit. A flash like a dying sun. White, blinding, and total. It hit them like a flash-bang—no heat, no fire—just sight ripped away and replaced.

For a heartbeat, no one could see. Not even Thane.

Just light. Followed by silence, and then the light faded, but not all at once—more like it was being pulled inward. Back into himself. Color seeped in slowly. Shapes returned. The cavern reassembled itself in shadow and stone.

And then they saw him.

Thane had collapsed against the far wall, half-slumped, where the moss still pulsed faintly with magic. His eyes were wide, unfocused, his chest heaving like he'd forgotten how to breathe. Blood ran in a slow, thin line from one ear, pooling on the neckline of this tunic.

His watch was dark again. Just a piece of glass.

Lirien reached him first. She dropped to her knees beside him, hands hovering before finally gripping his shoulders.

"Thane," she whispered. "Thane—can you hear me?"

He didn't answer. His gaze shifted slightly. Not quite recognition, more like he was *remembering* how to be human.

Behind them, the others began to stir.

Vesha dropped the machete, her hands still shaking. The blood on her robes had stopped flowing, but the memory of pain lingered on her face. She swayed where she stood, then staggered back a step, catching herself on the edge of a crate.

"What the hell was that?" Erynn murmured. "That wasn't magic. That was—"

"Wild Magic," Vesha cut in, still dazed. She looked toward the remains of the Saints. "But that's not what scares me."

She knelt, fingers brushing the tattered linen of the closest corpse. Her face had gone pale.

"These were Gutter Saints," she muttered. "They don't leave Devendor. They're Echo's… executioners. Priests. Seekers. Whatever he demands of them." Her fingers curled into fists. "They knew he was here. *But how?*"

"There's no time to guess," Lirien said sharply, helping Thane to his feet. He was barely able to stand, legs buckling, weight falling fully into her. "We have to go. Now."

Vesha nodded once, then again harder, forcing herself back to the moment. "Yes. Take him. Now that they've seen him, more will come. They won't stop."

Kaelir crossed to her side. His hand lifted, brushing against her cheek. Blood smeared across her skin from his fingers—his own, or hers, neither of them could tell.

"I thought I lost you," he said quietly.

Vesha didn't speak.

She just looked at him—really looked—and in that second, whatever had been held back between them unraveled. She closed her eyes, leaned in, and pulled him close.

Their lips met—brief, bruised, and utterly real.

When they parted, her breath caught against his.

"I'm still here," she whispered.

A pause.

Then somewhere above them, the ground shook. They widened their stances to keep their feet under them. Vesha's eyes darted upward.

"I must go help Aelith," she whispered. "You must protect him."

Kaelir swore softly. "Until we're out of time."

They moved quickly now—silent, practiced.

One by one, they retrieved their Breathstone masks from where they'd fallen. Kaelir looped his over his face with a practiced hand, the glassy stone humming faintly as it activated. Lirien followed, then Erynn—her fingers still trembling as she adjusted the strap over her hair.

Lirien turned to Thane. He hadn't moved since the light faded. His eyes still glassy, his breath shallow. Blood marked one ear and the corner of his lip.

"Thane." Her voice cut softly through the cavern. "We're going."

No response, but she didn't wait.

Sliding the mask over his face, she fastened it tight. The Breathstone pulsed once—reacting to him. Not with a hum this time, but with a flicker of blue-white light that danced like static across the glass.

Then she grabbed his arm and pulled it across her shoulders.

"I've got you."

She stepped to the edge of the dock, boots curling over the slippery moss. The water below didn't look like escape. It looked like a grave. But she didn't hesitate. With Thane's full weight draped across her, she plunged. The water took them with a hiss—*ice-cold* and merciless. Beneath the surface, darkness closed around them.

Thane's watch was the last light to fade, its face glowing pale gold. Then blood drifted into view, a faint swirl in the water, twisting past the glow.

And then darkness. Cold and complete.

9

BLOOD AND TEARS

Thane came to with a snap.

One second, nothing. The next, there were carpet fibers pressing into his cheek, the sour-slick taste of blood thick in his mouth. He blinked, dazed. Light pooled beneath the doorframe, and for a moment, he couldn't tell if it was morning or something worse.

His body was heavy, uncooperative. The weight of another world clung to his skin like static. He groaned, shifting just enough to bring his hand to his face. Wetness, but not his nose. It came from his ear. His fingers came back red, streaked with blood.

He rolled onto his side, coughing once—dry and sharp —then stilled as a voice drifted from down the hall.

"Thane?" His mother's voice, closer than expected. "Dr. Hughes just pulled up."

Shit.

He wiped the blood with his sleeve, panic rising. *The headset.* He twisted back, eyes locking on the battered VR rig still glowing faintly on the floor beside his mattress. The cable sparked once, then went dark.

He grabbed it and shoved it under his pillow.

The footsteps were moving down the hall, just outside his door now. Outside, the rain was pounding on the roof.

Thane fumbled for his cane where it had toppled near the wall. The tremble in his hands was worse again, both jittery and unpredictable. He hauled himself upright, forced weight into his legs, and limped toward the bathroom, dragging his foot slightly to keep the floor from creaking.

Looking back, the light spilling beneath the bedroom door felt foreign—too sharp, too real. He eased the door shut just as her footsteps stopped outside his bedroom.

Inside the bathroom, he flipped the faucet on and shoved his face under the stream. The water felt good, calming him. He soaked his hair and scrubbed at the blood, all while muttering curses under his breath like a ritual. Just something, anything, to remind him where he was.

Earth. It was always back to Earth.

The bathroom mirror was fogged from the steam, but he didn't look at it yet. He reached for a towel, wrapped it tight around his dripping hair, and cracked the bathroom door just as he saw his mom peeking into his room.

Her voice, gentler now. "Oh good, you're up."

Thane didn't look at her. Just mumbled, "Just showering," and then he let the bathroom door swing shut behind him again.

The bathroom mirror had cleared while he was toweling off. He caught a glimpse of himself—pale, hollow-eyed, water dripping down his neck—and nearly looked away. But something held him there.

From his bedroom, his mom's voice floated through the door. "Okay. Come on out. Dr. Hughes brought the test results."

He didn't answer.

He turned his wrist, looking at his watch, expecting it to still be frozen, but it wasn't. The second hand was ticking. Steady and measured—normal.

Too normal.

His chest tightened. The thing had been dead since Skyreach. Since the last time he'd died. He tapped the glass, but it didn't stop. It just kept ticking.

But why?

His thoughts flashed back to Thassriel. Back to the Alumata's dry voice in that candlelit archive, saying something about how time flowed differently now. That the world was unraveling. That *he* had changed.

"It's different there now," he whispered. Not to anyone. Not even to himself. Just to the empty air between worlds.

A sudden movement caught his eye. Reflected in the mirror—just behind him—three figures stood. Hunched and wrong. Their forms glitching at the edges like corrupted code, and they were staring straight at him.

The Gutter Saints.

He froze, heart hammering. Water dripped down his spine. Slowly—so slowly—all three raised an arm and pointed at him in eerie, synchronized silence.

Thane spun, hand scrabbling for the doorframe, but the was nothing. No one there. He turned back toward the mirror—only his own reflection remained. Pale and trembling.

His ears rang. Maybe from the blood. Maybe from something deeper, and he gripped the sink and stared himself down.

"You're not crazy," he said, jaw clenched. "You're not."

But the reflection didn't look convinced.

He stepped out of the bedroom and into the hallway, the towel still draped over his neck. The house felt smaller than usual. Quiet and still. He paused just outside the living room, half-shadowed by the hall.

His mother stood near the front door, one hand wrapped around a mug she wasn't drinking from. The other held her phone at her side, screen dark. She wasn't checking it. She wasn't doing anything, really, just standing there. Waiting.

Her shoulders sagged, and there was something brittle about her stillness. The kind of tension that came from clinging to good news that hadn't arrived yet—but still might.

Thane stared at her, throat tightening. She deserved to know. Deserved the truth about Arbelon. That it was real. That his father had been there—was still there. And about Echo.

He couldn't hold it back any longer. His mouth opened.

"Mom—"

The doorbell rang.

Jane flinched and the mug rattled in her hand.

Thane closed his mouth again. Saved and ruined. All at once.

The door opened with a familiar creak, and a breath of cold air followed it—wet and metallic with rain.

Dr. Hughes stepped inside, shoulders slightly hunched beneath his damp coat, raindrops clinging to his sleeves and darkening the cuffs. He paused on the doormat, removing his coat and wiping water droplets from his glasses, then offered a small nod as Jane ushered him in.

"Coffee?" she asked, already halfway to the kitchen.

He gave a tired smile and a small shake of the head. "No, thank you. I'll be up all night if I drink some now."

They made their way into the living room. Thane followed, stiff-legged, the ache in his joints worse than usual. He dropped onto the couch with a grunt and held his cane upright between his knees like a shield. Jane sat beside him, still clutching her mug like it was the only thing holding her together.

Dr. Hughes sat across from them, opening the folder with the kind of care that said he already knew what was inside.

"Your biomarkers," he began, voice measured, "suggest the treatment isn't taking. The rate of decline is…" He hesitated. "Unchanged. Possibly accelerating."

Silence pooled in the room like spilled ink.

Thane blinked once. "Accelerating?" he repeated, voice flat. "So we made it worse?"

"Please, Thane," Jane said softly.

Dr. Hughes adjusted his glasses. "It's not uncommon. These things can take time to stabilize before we see any real improvement. But Dr. Saito prepared a booster—an increase to the nanovirion load. It's experimental, but promising. We think it's the best chance at slowing things down."

"Of course it's experimental," Thane said, standing abruptly. Throwing his cane to the floor. "They always are. Aren't they?"

"Thane—" Jane started, reaching for him.

He leaned hard onto the back of the couch, moving to leave. "Why did I even agree to this? You know how many times I've heard that word—'promising'? It's just a lie. Everyone's lying to me."

Dr. Hughes said nothing.

Jane rose slowly, eyes locked on her son. "He believed in this work—your father—it was his life's work. He believed it would change everything. I know it will work. Just give it a chance."

And there it was.

Thane's breath caught. A quiet, bitter laugh slipped through his teeth. "That's not fair… don't bring him into this."

"I'm just saying," Jane said, her voice trembling, "he wouldn't have wanted you to give up."

He turned away, jaw tight.

She was unraveling. He could hear it in the shake of her voice. See it in the way she clutched her mug like it might shatter. He knew the truth already: it wouldn't help him. Not really.

But maybe it would help her. And somehow, that became enough to continue with this charade. He sat back down, rolled up his sleeve, and extended his arm toward Dr. Hughes. His eyes didn't leave his mother's face.

"Hit me, Doc," he said, the bitterness sharp in his throat.

Dr. Hughes moved without a word, withdrawing a small vial from the kit beside him. The label was hand-written.

Booster 1A.

He loaded the syringe, careful and practiced, like he'd done this hundreds of times, but there was something in the way his hands moved. Slower and heavier, like he didn't want to do it either.

Thane didn't flinch when the needle slid in. He didn't even look. His eyes stayed fixed on his mother, unblinking. The sting was sharp, then dull. A subtle warmth spread through his arm, too faint to trust. Too soon to mean anything.

Jane exhaled beside him, barely more than a breath. "This is going to work," she said. Her voice cracked on the last word. "It has to."

No one answered. Not Dr. Hughes. Not Thane. And the silence that followed was complete. Except for the rain, it kept pounding on the roof like none of this had happened.

Thane grabbed his cane from the floor and stood without a word. He didn't look at either of them. Didn't say goodbye. He just turned and shuffled toward the hallway, his gait uneven, the quiet thunk of the cane barely masking the drag of his foot on the floor. His hands trembled worse now—worse than they had in weeks—and he gripped the cane harder to hide it.

His bedroom door clicked shut behind him. He locked it out of habit more than defiance.

Inside, everything felt smaller. The headset was still tucked under his pillow. He pulled it out, cradled it in his hands like something sacred and broken. Cracks spidered through the casing. Wires exposed at the seams. It looked more corpse than conduit.

His breath finally settled.

"If he found a way out," Thane whispered, "maybe I can too."

His eyes drifted to the photo on the nightstand. His father—younger, smiling, alive—still in his lab coat, arm slung over a chalkboard filled with equations Thane had never understood, and likely never would. It all looked like hope, or maybe just an empty memory.

He raised the headset. But just before he put it on, a sharp tick broke the silence. It was his watch. The face was glowing again—no longer steady. Electrical glitches danced across the screen in fragmented sparks. Then, underneath the distortion, a low hum began to rise.

Not outside. *Inside.*

His breath caught. It wasn't just sound. It was pressure. A resonance that echoed in the marrow of his skull, like a tuning fork struck too close to the brainstem. The nanovirions were responding. Searching.

And something was answering.

The hum deepened and tightened.

Then Echo's voice ground out. But it wasn't a hallucination or a memory this time. It was something else. Something intimate.

"You cling to hope for her. But you've seen what's waiting in Arbelon—let me show you the way."

The words weren't in the air. They were *in* him, coiling through his thoughts like wire and smoke, threading themselves between his memories and fear. A channel, open and alive, not a dream. No, this was too visceral, too concrete.

Thane's jaw clenched. He pressed his palm to his temple like he could crush the signal with pressure alone.

"Get out of my head," he hissed.

There was a pause, and then a softer, almost gentle response.

"You came back. You'll always come back."

Another pause, a moment too long. Then…

"You have no other option now."

The watch pulsed again—not light, but in response. A rhythmic flicker behind the numbers, like a heartbeat answering a call.

He stared at it. And for the first time, he wondered—maybe the booster was working—strengthening the connection.

He blinked once. Then, slowly, deliberately, he raised the headset again, the familiar weight of it fitting awkwardly in his hands, colder than it should've been.

One last breath. Then he lowered the rig over his head. The interior padding smelled faintly of dust and sweat and something else—something sharp beneath the surface. Static.

Thane clenched his jaw and shut his eyes.
It's time for some answers.
Click.
Flash.
Darkness.

10

————

DARK PLACES

THERE WAS NOTHING.

No sound. No sight. Only pressure, cold and crushing.

Thane came to in darkness with something strapped over his face. Tight. Humming.

He couldn't breathe.

Pitch-black water pressed in from every side. His limbs hung loose, weightless, but not free. His chest convulsed, begging for air, but all he drew in was the thin mechanical rattle of whatever clung to his mouth. It felt like waking up buried alive again—only this time, the coffin was made of water.

A grip clamped tight around him. A body, pressed to his like iron. A presence. A force holding him in place, holding him under.

Was it dragging him down?

He panicked. His body twisted, and he kicked out wild and unhinged, but the grip on him was unrelenting. He wasn't moving forward, he was sinking. Drowning. Dying. And still, the pressure grew tighter, the hold on him firmer.

The mask on his face resisted every breath that now came thin and wheezing. It wasn't enough air.

He reached up and tore at it. Cold fingers slipping over slick stone and leather. It finally came loose, and the river answered. Water surged up his nose, down his throat, and his body bucked. He tried to scream, but all that came out was air—and then nothing.

He thrashed harder. The thing holding him wouldn't let go. It wasn't arms anymore, it was coils. More like shackles or tentacles. Something that wouldn't let go. His mind scrambled for meaning, for air, for *escape*.

Above him, as if this could get any stranger, something brushed his forehead. It felt like a snake. He bucked harder. His feral instincts released. He wanted to live, but he was sinking. From the dark, his wristwatch flickered. A dim pulse. Then another, but the face glitched, the hands moving forward and back. But it was the only light, the only proof that he existed at all.

He was in darkness, only a small bubble of light. There was no surface, no sky. No up, no down. No Earth, no Arbelon.

Just black. Just pressure.

His mind clawed for logic, but found none. This wasn't a glitch. He knew this wasn't a dream. It wasn't anything he knew. It was something worse.

Then the grip on him changed. It shifted from something monstrous to something... steady. Steady, and pulling. A moment later, cool air hit his skin, the chill settling deeper into his bones. He'd breached into a pocket of space where the ceiling arched just high enough to keep the water from swallowing it.

As his head broke the surface, he let out a strangled gasp. He sucked in too fast and too hard, coughing violently, body thrashing as he tore away from the presence behind him.

"Thane… stop…" Lirien's voice cut through the splash and flailing. "It's me. Just breathe."

He didn't hear her at first. Didn't care. He shoved away, arms churning at the water. His back hit stone—slick and curved. Only then did he pause, chest heaving, pupils wide. His mask glowed faintly on his forehead.

His breath burned going in. Cold and wet and real. Then he heard her voice again, but this time it landed. Lirien was next to him, treading the same water. Her hair clung to her face, her voice low but sharp.

"You done?" she asked, a bit unkindly.

He didn't answer, just turned and coughed hard into the crook of his arm, still gulping air like it was a drug.

The others surfaced seconds later—Kaelir, then Erynn —each gasping and shivering. Kaelir stayed quiet, eyes scanning the ceiling. Erynn floated with both arms stretched up, gripping the chain pulley just to hold herself steady.

It took minutes for their breathing to calm. The cavern echoed with it—wet breath, shivers, dripping stone, and little else. No light beyond the faintest glow from their Breathstones, barely visible now that their use had subsided. But Thane's wristwatch had gone dark. It wasn't ticking or pulsing, just silent.

He glanced around the space, then muttered, "Where the fuck are we?"

Nothing registered. Just cold black water and half a breath left in him.

Lirien floated beside him, expression flat. "Still traveling the river. Out of Felderwin."

She paused, and her tone sharpened. "And you're welcome, by the way."

Thane blinked at her, and then looked down, sheepish. "Yeah... Okay... Sorry about that."

"You better be," she answered between shivers.

Kaelir checked the group silently, hands brushing shoulders, eyes on every breath. Erynn didn't say anything, she floated silent among them, her eyes closed, breathing slowly.

They were all soaked, exhausted, half-frozen. For a long moment, no one spoke. The water stilled around them. Only the drip of the cavern ceiling and the low hum of their masks marked the reality of the world around them.

Then Lirien leaned close to Thane. "We made it," she said quietly. "You're alright. Okay?"

Thane nodded, still catching his breath.

"...Yeah," he whispered.

"Let's go then," Lirien said.

She was the first to dip beneath the surface again—effortless, efficient. The chain gave a soft tug as she pulled forward.

One by one, they followed.

Their Breathstone masks slid back into place with a hiss. Thane hesitated, but forced it over his face. The stone was cold against his skin, humming to life.

Beneath the surface, the tunnel dipped. Then widened. Then dipped and widened again. They were in and out of full submersion. It took some time to work their way down the river, but eventually, they surfaced into a space so vast it stole what little breath they had left. A cathedral hollowed out beneath the surface of the world, carved from stone, with a vaulted ceiling high above that allowed just enough filtered light to keep the edges from being wholly swallowed in shadow. In the distance, they could see the surface of the river flowed out of an opening into the sunlight in the world beyond.

Turning his head, Thane saw stone docks that lined the left edge of the cavern. Thick pillars towered above them like forgotten guardians. Crates lay stacked in moldering heaps, furred with mildew and webbed like tombs. Faded signage clung to the wall above three gated archways carved into the stone of the docks:

MERCHANT STORAGE ONLY

A dilapidated ferry rocked gently near the dock, half of its deck covered in rot. Smaller boats floated nearby, some cracked and waterlogged, others leaning into each other like huddled ghosts.

They drifted into the space in silence, the current barely moving them as they peeled the Breathstones off.

Kaelir's voice came soft. "These were trade tunnels. Before the river rose. Before the collapse."

No one answered. The weight of the space hung around them. It was a lost place, a distant memory beneath the city—a port no one above remembered, rotting quietly in the dark.

Erynn floated to the ferry, catching the edge of the railing. She tested it with one foot. The deck groaned, but didn't give, so she climbed aboard.

"It'll do," she said, water streaming from her hair.

Kaelir followed without a word, pulling himself up after her. The boat dipped under his weight, sending a splash over the edge.

Erynn glared at him as she worked to steady herself. "Really?"

Kaelir didn't answer. He just moved to the rudder and began checking the oarlocks.

Thane floated beside them, staring at the stone arches in the distance. Moss hung from the carved lintels like damp hair. Everything felt so… forgotten.

Erynn climbed to the bow of the ferry, water sloshing around her boots as she bent low and pulled the soaked satchel from beneath her cloak. Her hands trembled—part from cold, part from nerves. She opened the flap slowly and rummaged through it. Then pulled free a tightly rolled scroll, tied with faded blue twine.

Her map. Thane recognized it instantly. The annotated map of the Arbelon. She'd worked on it during every quiet moment since they met, sketching notes, marking warnings, measuring distances—all coded with annotations and symbols in the margins.

She untied it and unrolled it. Ink ran in feathery veins across the parchment. Entire regions bled into each other. Mountains had become bruises. Tributaries smeared like cracks in glass. The main river still curved south, but everything else was gone.

"Damn it…" she whispered.

Kaelir stepped beside her. He looked, then nodded.

"We still know the river runs south to Swain," he said. "It'll guide us."

Erynn didn't respond. Just stared a moment longer, then began folding it back, slowly, like it hurt. But before the map vanished into her satchel, she paused. Another shape rested at the bottom of the pack, and she pulled it free.

The Codex.

Even from a distance, Thane could see the damage. Its leather cover was swollen and warped. Pages stuck together in pulpy clumps. Ink had run like oil through parchment. Names, dates, references, all blurred to nothing.

She flipped it open and tried to separate two pages, but they tore.

"No, no, no…" she breathed, voice cracking. "Please."

She gripped the Codex tighter, like she could will it back to life. Like pressure could save it.

Thane watched, unsure what to say. Then found something, knowing it sounded cliché.

"Things can be replaced," he said softly. "People can't. And we're still here."

Erynn didn't respond, her jaw twitching.

Kaelir looked up at Thane, expression unreadable, but there was something in his eyes. Surprise, agreement, maybe both.

"Yes," he said. "And we still have what matters. The path forward."

Erynn didn't look at either of them. She just held the ruined Codex to her chest, and nodded. But tears slipped down her cheeks anyway.

At the rudder, Lirien's voice came quiet.

"We need to keep moving. It's not safe here."

No one argued, and in the next instant they pushed off in silence. The ferry rocked faintly as Kaelir eased it from the dock. The oarlocks groaned in protest, then fell into a rhythm, his slow strokes guiding them into the current.

The air grew colder. Above them, the roof of the cavern narrowed, pinched tight into a dark tunnel, and then it thrust them out onto the open water of the Andriel where the current pulled them forward. The river was deep and slow, but not still. Its current whispered beneath the boat like breath under a closed door, constant, patient, and unrelenting. The sound of it dissipated into the air around them.

Somewhere above, far to the west, the sun was well on its way to setting. The light filtering through the trees that lined the banks, fading to nothing. The only glow came from the crescent moon that sat low in the sky, faint and reluctant.

Thane stared at his watch. Whatever Thassriel had done, he'd fixed it. It was ticking again, steady and normal. He stared at it for a long time. The pulse was exact. Unbroken. Every second clean, but still somehow unnatural.

He glanced to the riverbanks. Forest and brush greeted the water's edge. Through the shadows, an occasional flicker of something more—figures, maybe, or shapes. They flickered in and out, there for a moment, then not. Sometimes the branches looked too crisp, like someone had drawn them too sharply in one corner and forgotten the others. Sometimes the river ahead loaded just quick enough, like the world was building itself just far enough ahead to meet their pace, and falling apart behind them as the ferry slid further south down the river.

Thane leaned back, holding the silence of the moment, and the others followed suit. The silence grew heavier the farther they went, but it wasn't tense, it was a welcome break from the intensity of the battle and the fractured escape below Felderwin.

But the silence couldn't hold, and eventually, Thane broke it.

"What do we know about this Swain place?"

Erynn looked up. She hadn't moved much. The Codex still sat in her lap like a wound. Her fingers traced the cover.

"Not much," she murmured. "Old traveler's warnings. Places to avoid. You know… that sort of thing."

Kaelir didn't look up. "Nothing confirmed. Just fragments. The kind of stories that make you go somewhere else instead."

"Well, that's not ominous at all," Thane muttered.

No one disagreed.

The current carried them on. Kaelir had taken the rudder, quiet and watchful. Lirien faced forward, her eyes half-closed, breath slow, while Erynn traced her fingers across the ruined pages. Over and over, like she could summon the memory of them.

And Thane just stared into the dark. Still there. Still broken.

The current slackened as dawn broke... or what *passed* for dawn. Mist curled over the surface of the water, thick and low, clinging to the hull as if trying to hold them back. The river bent once—then again—and spilled them into a narrow inlet snaking through the forest, where a crooked wooden dock jutted from the bank.

Kaelir dipped an oar to slow them. The boat drifted to a stop with a hollow scrape of wood against wood.

"We're here," he said quietly, jumping ashore.

Swain waited just beyond, nestled into the trees. The others hauled themselves off the rotting ferry. The air was warmer here. Still damp, but thick with the scent of sweet-grass, morning bread, and chimney smoke.

As they walked off the dock, the village emerged like a painting, but too vivid and precise. Sunlight caught on painted shutters and thatched rooftops, bouncing in ways light rarely should. The buildings were cheerful, colorful, almost *charming*, each one distinct with hand-touches, lined with bright trims and iron lanterns. Gardens overflowed with flowers. Ivy climbed in perfect spirals. Wind-chimes tinkled.

A cobbler stepped outside and stretched.

A butcher in a bloodied apron waved.

A group of laughing children chased a flock of startled chickens through the town square.

From somewhere down the lane, a baker whistled as he passed by, his basket full of steaming loaves, dropping them into waiting baskets at each cottage. But the tune never changed. It was the same, over and over, like it had nowhere else to go.

A man loading a cart with firewood turned as they approached, and his face lit up.

"Welcome, travelers! You've arrived safely, thank the Watchers!"

He smiled. Warm and genuine.

Thane turned, but the man seemed to rewind—loading the same wood. Still smiling. Then, half a breath later, it looped again.

"Welcome, travelers! You've arrived safely, thank the Watchers!"

Same words. Same tone. Same smile.

Everyone froze, even Kaelir.

Then Thane looked up, just in time to see a cat leap from a rooftop to a low garden wall. Then it did it again.

Same arc. Same tail flick. Same motion.

Looping.

Lirien took a step forward. Her hand drifted toward her dagger, but not to draw it, just to *touch* it.

"Things seem… *broken* here," she said softly.

Erynn's voice was a whisper. "That matches the stories. But I never believed they could be true."

Thane looked between them, slow and deliberate. "So you can *see* it? Finally? The glitches."

Lirien didn't answer, but Kaelir's jaw tensed. His eyes scanned the village again, only slower now. More measured.

"Yes," Kaelir said. "This isn't right."

A dog barked in the distance. Then again. Same pitch. Same cadence.

The baker passed again. Still whistling. Still the same tune.

They stepped forward into the square. Closer now, they could see a handful of market stalls arranged along the cobbled walk. Wood-framed awnings draped in cheerful colors. Barrels stacked with dried grains and nuts. Fresh herbs braided in hanging bunches. The scent of citrus and cardamom mingled with smoke and earth.

One stall in particular caught the eye—heaped high with overripe fruit. Apples in glossy pyramids. Oranges stacked with impossible symmetry. Berries mounded like gemstones in shallow wooden trays. The whole thing looked like it had been staged for a painting, but then left out too long in the sun.

A man stood behind the stall, sleeves rolled to the elbow, fingers stained berry-dark. He looked up and beamed.

"Well, look at *you* lot," he said, voice chipper and strange. "Been a long while since we've had visitors! Come to browse, have you? Got the finest fruit this side of the river!"

Erynn stepped forward cautiously. Her boots squelched faintly on the mossy stones. "We're looking for a way through," she said, polite but measured. "To Faelenshara."

The man's eyes lit up, too fast. "Ahhh… come looking for the crossing, did you?" he said, rubbing his hands together. "Well! That's a tricky sort of business, isn't it? Not everyone comes asking for that. You'll be wanting to talk to Orren."

"Orren?" Kaelir asked from behind her, voice low.

"Lovely fellow," the man said brightly. "Keeps to himself, mostly. But he knows these woods better than anyone. You'll find him down by the falls. Never leaves, really. The whole place is sort of his… domain."

He turned and gestured casually toward a trail beside the riverbank, barely visible through the trees. Mist clung to the underbrush. The sound of distant water echoed—steady, like breath.

"Follow that," he said. "You'll find the falls. And Orren."

Thane stepped forward, arms crossed. "And if he can't help us?" he asked. "Or won't?"

The man blinked.

Then blinked again.

And then he laughed, bright and tinny, like someone had pressed play on a soundbite. "Oh, don't be silly," he said, too cheerfully. "That doesn't happen!"

Behind him, a woman carrying a tray of mushrooms had stopped mid-step. Her smile hadn't changed. Neither had her eyes.

Another man, leaning on a broom, stood behind her, frozen for a moment too long before slowly beginning to sweep again… from the same spot he'd already cleared.

Thane didn't move, but something behind his ribs twitched. "Of course it doesn't," he muttered.

The fruit seller just smiled wider. "And if you get turned around," the man added, still beaming, "don't worry—we'll be right here."

Everyone nodded in response, wide-eyed. Except for Kaelir, who leaned closer to Erynn. "We should go."

Lirien was already moving toward the path by the river, one hand still near her belt. "Yes," she agreed. "Right now."

They moved in unison without another word. As they stepped out of the square and onto the mist-wrapped path toward the falls, the fruit-seller raised a hand behind them in parting.

"Safe travels!" he called. "We'll see you again real soon!"

The words echoed. Too perfectly, as if they'd been said before, and would be said again.

They followed the path in silence. The sound of the village faded behind them—muffled laughter, barking dogs, a child's voice calling out again. And again. And again.

The trail bent gently toward the river. Mist clung to the undergrowth in soft curls, rising in tendrils that danced around their boots. The trees on either side leaned inward, not unnaturally, but just enough to feel intentional. As if the forest wanted them to stay on the path and not stray.

Up ahead, the rush of falling water grew louder, and behind them, Swain kept looping.

Thane glanced back once.

The square was barely visible through the trees, but the line was clear enough to see the same boy chasing the same chicken, again. Same squeal. Same laughter. Same stumble.

The fruit vendor waving at them. Still smiling. Still creepy.

Thane turned away, quickening his pace, and he didn't look back again.

The path dipped through a break in the trees, the river running to their right now—wider here, slower. Shadows flickered across its surface, too deep for the light.

Then they saw it. The waterfall rose above the trees. It poured like glass from a fractured granite ledge, a smooth sheet tumbling down and disappearing into the canopy below. The sound was constant—soothing, almost—though beneath it, something else thrummed.

Thane paused and looked toward the falls. The whole area had a strange shimmer to it, subtle, but unmistakable, like heat rising off pavement on a hot summer day. The light twisted around the waterfall, bending and folding in the air.

He blinked. Then it was gone.

There was only one thing left to do, so he stepped forward with the others.

Toward the falls.

11

THE PRICE OF PASSAGE

THE PATH gently curled upward in slow, deliberate switchbacks, each step taking them deeper into a hush that felt almost sacred. The trees grew stranger here—tall and sinuous, their branches arching toward one another like cathedral vaults, draped in moss that shimmered faintly with a dew that never fell. Beneath their feet, the trail was edged with ferns and padded with fallen leaves so deep it felt conjured.

Somewhere ahead, they heard the roar of water. It wasn't the chaotic sound of a flood or a storm, but more akin to a steady voice, constant and low, like the whisper of something ancient remembering itself.

Thane moved near the rear of the group, quiet. He hadn't said much since Swain. No one had. Not really. But even in the silence, his legs screamed from the climb. As they reached the rise, the sun broke through. Then the forest fell away, suddenly and all at once, opening into a wide clearing bathed in golden light and silver spray.

The waterfall cascaded down a sheer cliff-face, white and endless, splitting at the bottom into a crescent-shaped pool that was emerald blue and rimmed in a white lime-stone. Sunlight pierced the mist and scattered into fractured rainbows. The air smelled of wet granite and green leaves, sharp and clean, like a new memory.

A small stone cottage sat tucked against the cliff—low-slung and moss-covered, with a wooden door standing open and a chimney puffing thin trails of smoke into the sky.

Thane came to a stop beside Lirien, her gaze drifting over the falls. "It's beautiful," she said quietly.

Kaelir said nothing. His jaw was set, eyes scanning the tree-line, the water, the cottage. Always checking. Always weighing.

"Look," Erynn murmured, pointing toward the pool.

A man crouched near the water's edge, hands submerged to the wrists, as if testing the temperature or listening to something beneath the surface. His robes were pale and tailored finely at the hems, and his long silver hair spilled around his shoulders, like the waterfall itself. He turned toward them, slow and deliberate. Then he smiled.

"Welcome," he called out, his voice warm and even. "You've come far."

He stood, water dripping from his fingers, and brushed a lock of hair behind one ear. The movement was graceful, but there was a weight behind it, like he moved in time with something older than himself. Something about him felt as still and unmoving as a stone beneath the water—ancient, patient, and utterly immovable.

Thane narrowed his eyes. He didn't know who this man was, but he already didn't trust him.

The man approached with easy grace, robes whispering as he walked. He stopped a few paces from the group, just far enough that his presence didn't press—yet somehow, it still filled the clearing.

"If you wish," he said, gesturing to the mossy stones arranged in a loose half-circle near the water's edge. "You may sit and rest. That climb is not a kind one. I've done it too many times myself."

No one moved at first, but then Lirien nodded once and stepped forward, settling on one of the stones. Erynn followed, then Thane. Kaelir remained standing, arms crossed, his gaze never leaving the man.

The stranger retrieved a small satchel from beneath a root, producing a bundle wrapped in cloth. He unwrapped it slowly, revealing slices of dried fruit and something dark and leathery, possibly jerky. He placed it all on a flat stone between them. From a wooden jug, he poured water into clay cups carved with strange sigils Thane didn't recognize.

"I am called Orren," he said. "The trees and the forest provides what it can. I make use of it to the best of my ability. Please enjoy," he said, motioning to them.

Erynn gave a polite nod and took a piece of dried fruit. Lirien sipped her water, but Thane didn't move.

"What brings travelers to my falls?" he asked. "I have few visitors from the outside these days."

His eyes passed over the group, finally landing on Thane for an uncomfortable span of time. There was something in the look, a soft curiosity, but also something more.

No one answered right away.

Erynn's fingers paused around her cup. "We were sent by Thassriel."

Orren stood looking at the falls, swirling the water in his cup.

They all looked on in silence.

"Now that is a name I've not heard in some time," Orren said, turning back. "He sent you here, to Swain?"

"He did," Erynn answered, regaining her confidence.

"Swain," Orren said, lifting his glass and taking a sip. "That place has not slept properly in years." His words were gentle, but they landed like a needle beneath the skin, and the silence that followed thickened.

Orren turned his gaze on Thane. It wasn't aggressive, just… curious.

"And yet, you *saw* it, didn't you?" he asked. "Most pass through and never notice. They nod along to the rhythm. Smile at the loop. But you…" His voice slowed. "You saw something else, beneath it. That alone makes you different…"

Thane didn't answer. He didn't need to.

Orren's eyes narrowed faintly in something like respect —or warning. "Dangerous, maybe. Or cursed."

Thane bristled. His mouth opened to speak, but Erynn cleared her throat, careful with her words.

"We seek passage," she said softly. "Through the Veil. To Faelenshara."

The shift was immediate. Orren's hands stilled. He set his cup down, took a cloth, and dried them slowly, deliberately—each finger, each knuckle. Then he folded it and set it down beside the dried fruit.

His smile faded.

"Faelenshara is closed."

He said it simply. No anger. No sorrow. Just truth.

"You may rest here. But then you must be on your way."

The silence that followed pulled taut like a drawn bowstring. Thane's hands curled at his sides, and Kaelir opened his mouth to speak, but Orren spoke first, his gaze sharp and still as the pool.

"Don't misunderstand me," Orren interrupted, voice still level. "But most who find this place do so by mistake.

Those who come with purpose..." He looked between them. "Rarely understand the cost."

Kaelir took a step forward. Not rushing, just enough to break the line.

"We don't have time for your riddles," he said, voice low but edged like a drawn blade. "The world is burning behind us. If you're waiting for us to beg, you'll be waiting a while."

Orren didn't flinch. He looked up at Kaelir, expression unreadable, then shifted slightly.

"Your kind always thinks lighting something on fire makes you righteous," he said flatly to Kaelir. Then his eyes turned to Thane.

"But the last time this kind of magic appeared," he said, voice colder now, "it brought ruin."

Thane froze.

Orren took a step closer—not threatening, but resolute.

"That magic inside you," he said. "It is unnatural. I've only seen it once before. It bloomed in the veins of a dying man who should've never crossed the Veil. His madness fed the Rending."

Something in Thane's chest twisted. His fists clenched.

"You don't know anything about my father."

"Your father?" Erynn and Lirien gasped almost in unison.

"What are you talking about?" Lirien whispered, her eyes flitting between Thane and Orren.

Orren met Thane's gaze, and for the first time, there was a glint of something raw in his eyes.

"Oh, are we keeping secrets?"

"Shut up," Thane snapped, the words rawer than he meant them to be.

"I was there," Orren continued cooly. "I know he left

scars that still bleed." He paused. "If you carry the same fire, I will not let you pass."

Kaelir's hand moved to the hilt at his side. His voice snapped like flint. "Then maybe you'll bleed first."

Orren raised a hand. Behind him, the surface of the pool twitched violently.

"The border was left unguarded once. Never again. Not while I still breathe."

Orren stepped backward, into the pool. The water accepted him without resistance, swirling around his legs like it knew him. Then it lifted. Not splashing—rising. Controlled. Reverent. Liquid gathered at his shoulders, then surged upward in graceful coils, wrapping his limbs, his chest. A translucent armor formed over his robe, woven from water and light. Sigils shimmered faintly across the surface, shifting with each breath. In one hand, the water coalesced into a blade like molten glass, rippling with faint currents. In the other, a broad, curved shield erupted from the surface of the pool, shaped like a falling wave.

The clearing had changed. The birds went silent. The mist thickened, rolling inward from the trees, and the air turned damp and heavy with power. The light dimmed, not from clouds, but as if the forest itself had narrowed its gaze.

Orren's voice deepened, carrying far more than sound, something older stirred behind it.

"You stand at the border of Faelenshara," he intoned. "You will not pass while I still draw breath."

He lifted the blade slightly, just enough for it to catch the light and fracture it into colorless fire.

"No one crosses the Veil unchanged. If blood is not paid—memory will be."

The mist stirred again. Water curled around Kaelir's boots. Lirien shifted, her hand brushing Thane's arm, not in fear, but grounding. Getting ready for whatever was to come.

The forest held its breath, and the pool rippled once more.

Kaelir drew his sword, about to step forward as Lirien pushed her way in front of him, stopping his progress.

Kaelir froze, his blade half-raised.

"Enough," Lirien said, stepping fully between them. Her palms hovered in the air, one hand toward Orren, the other toward Kaelir. "This is nonsense." Her voice was calm, but it cut clean through the rising storm.

The mist stirred again, as if unsure what to do next.

Erynn moved beside her, breath quick but steady. She didn't raise her voice, but there was a clarity in it now, a resolve honed sharp by purpose.

"You know that Thassriel sent us," she said, eyes locked on Orren. "Not for conquest. Not to steal. We came because the world is breaking. The Heart of Arbelon is failing, and if it fails, so does everything else."

Orren's blade remained raised, but he didn't speak.

"The Heart isn't a weapon," Erynn continued, her voice trembling now, just slightly. "It's the last light of our dying world. And we're not here to watch it fade. We came to do something. To be more than a witness to its fall."

She paused, chest rising with each breath, then added quietly. "You said blood or memory must be paid. Then we choose memory."

Silence followed. Deep and real. Orren's form didn't move, but the mist around him thinned slightly. The blade in his hand dimmed.

Then a voice echoed from behind the falls, low and almost melodic.

"So be it," it said. "Memory it is, then."

All eyes turned toward the waterfall.

From the shimmering wall of water, a figure stepped through—barefoot and dry despite the torrent behind him. Petals swirled around his feet like a drifting tide. His robes matched Orren's in color and cut, but where Orren's presence was stone, this man was breath and light, wrapped in vapor.

He walked slowly toward the pool, eyes resting on Orren.

"Brother."

"Nerro," Orren said, exhaling, long and slow, lowering his blade.

The armor that wrapped Orren's body cracked—not with force, but grace—and fell away into droplets, sinking back into the pool. The shield followed, dissolving into quiet ripples. Then the air lightened, the mist receded, and then the two Fae stood there, side by side. Identical twins.

Nerro held his hands out, palms facing up. His voice didn't rise, but it carried with strange weight.

"One memory each," he said. "That is the price. The Veil will determine if its value is worthy, so choose wisely."

The surface of the pool rippled again behind him, as if in quiet agreement.

He stepped toward Erynn first.

"Are you prepared to make the sacrifice?"

Erynn stood Stoic, nodding.

Nerro raised his hands. The water followed, arching upward, curling like fingers. A ribbon of water lifted toward her brow. She didn't flinch, and the moment it touched her, she gasped—not in pain, but in recognition. Her eyes flickered, then settled. Nerro held a hand beneath the ribbon as it condensed into a small crystal vial, faintly glowing.

Then he turned to Lirien. She swallowed, then nodded. The water touched her skin, and her breath caught in her throat. When it withdrew, something fragile lingered in her expression. Another small crystal vial, faintly glowing.

Kaelir's was next. He stood tall, jaw tight, eyes forward. The water touched him. Unlike the others, he didn't blink, but when it pulled away, his hands trembled—just once. Nerro caught the memory, sealing it into another vial, this one darker than the rest.

Then he turned to Thane.

The water hesitated. Then rose, slow and certain.

Thane stiffened, his body already reacting before the water made contact. When it touched his forehead, the watch at his wrist flickered—just once. A shimmer of static traced the metal. Then heat lanced down his spine, sharp and invasive. His vision flared white, but it wasn't light. It was loss, a hollowing. A subtraction. Something pulled from behind his eyes.

Nerro's face tightened—not with effort, but surprise.

"This one holds tightly," he murmured.

The water pulsed and Thane staggered back a step, teeth gritted. The ribbon of water snapped taut, but the memory finally came loose. Nerro caught it in his palm, then slowly let it condense into a crystalline vial.

Thane blinked. He tried to recall what he'd given, but there was nothing. Only static. A smear where something used to be. Whatever it was, it was just gone like it never existed.

Nerro turned back toward the pool and lifted the vials high. There were four in total—each a different hue, each humming faintly with something unseen.

He looked to Orren.

"The Veil accepts the offering."

Orren stepped forward once more. No armor now, only robes and bare hands. He dipped two fingers into the pool and lifted them to Erynn's forehead. A glowing sigil bloomed on her skin—brief and beautiful, then faded into nothing.

One by one, he marked them all.

When he reached Thane, the sigil shimmered longer than the others, reluctant to vanish. It sizzled faintly before sinking into his skin.

"This is the Mark of Truth," Orren said. "In Faelen-shara, you will speak only what is real. Lies will burn."

Nerro's voice followed softly behind.

"Or worse."

The mist parted and Orren stepped aside without a word. He no longer stood as a sentinel, but as something gentler. Something resigned to now let them pass.

"Where I guard, he guides," Orren said, gesturing to his brother. "You will go with him now. He will take you to the Lady. She will judge your worth... and measure your intents."

He knelt at the pool's edge, dipping his hand into the water once again. A pulse of light rippled from his fingers, spreading outward in slow, concentric rings. From the surface, a bridge emerged—not stone or wood, but water made solid by intent and magic. It shimmered with each ripple, arcing gently across the pool toward the base of the waterfall. Mist swirled where it touched, catching the light like fractured glass.

Nerro turned to them, the vials of memory tucked into a pouch at his side.

"A memory given freely," he said, "is more binding than any oath."

He looked at each of them in turn. "Come. The Lady waits."

No one spoke, but Thane's legs moved before his mind did—his feet stepping onto the bridge like a sleepwalker.

The water held firm beneath his boots, humming faintly with each step. The others followed, single file, behind him. Nerro took the lead.

As they crossed, the roar of the waterfall dimmed—not into silence, but into something stranger. Voices. Not in language, but in *feeling*—like someone whispering memories into the back of their thoughts. A laugh half-forgotten. A touch from someone long dead. Echoes of old warmth. Old wounds.

Thane's head buzzed. He didn't look back. Behind them, Orren watched them go. His expression unreadable, but as Nerro neared the edge of the falls, he turned, and met his brother's eyes.

No words passed between them, only a look. Shared history. Shared burden.

Then Nerro turned away.

They stepped through the waterfall. Not into water, but into something else. The veil shimmered around them— light bending, air thickening, the world folding like a page turned too quickly. For a moment, it was all color and cold and pressure, and then they emerged.

Dry.

But the world had changed. The forest on this side of the falls pulsed with an otherworldly bloom. Trees rose taller, bending like dancers mid-bow. Moss glowed softly violet beneath their feet, illuminating a narrow path flanked by vines that glimmered faintly, like veins of starlight.

Nerro stood at the edge of the trail, waiting.

He didn't speak. He just turned and they followed.

1 2

THORNS OF THE WYRD

MIST COILED LOW across the glade, not silver now, but stained in hues that didn't belong to either day or night. The light here was strange, like it had been over-saturated, each color too sharp, too rich. Leaves shone with impossible greens, shadows pulsed violet at the edges, and blooms caught the light like living prisms. Where the trees opened, they stepped into something quieter than silence, like the forest itself was holding its breath.

This was Faelenshara.

It shimmered, even in the shadows. Every leaf was edged in soft fractals of light, every petal catching glimmers that danced in and out of view. Some blooms hung upside down like lamps, some pulsed like breathing lungs, others looked too much like open eyes to be comforting. And the ground didn't feel like ground. There was no dirt or roots. Only a soft loam that hide their footsteps, as if the forest itself was alive beneath their feet.

None of them spoke. Even Kaelir's usual scowl had softened into something distant, marked with a childish wonder. Lirien walked beside Thane, close but not touch-

125

ing. Her gaze flicked over the trees as if reading a language none of them knew. Erynn, for once, didn't look eager. She looked complete.

But Thane hated how beautiful this place was. How fragile it looked. It reminded him of things he didn't want to feel.

And then she arrived.

Not with trumpets or fanfare. She was just there. A figure taking shape in the mist ahead, stepping out between two trees whose trunks curved like tusks, spreading wide on her approach. Her steps made no sound. Her gown—if it was a gown—trailed like silk woven from fog and starlight.

Her face hurt to look at. Not from ugliness. From the opposite.

She wore masks, layered and shimmering—transparent and shifting, one atop the next like petals of emotion. Joy. Sorrow. Rage. Curiosity. A flicker of despair. A flicker of something else. They slid over her skin like oil on water, but when their eyes tried to pin her down, the masks stilled, and she became one thing—beautiful. And terribly so.

And her voice—when it came—was worse. It rang like a memory of music. Like a song you forgot, but still knew by heart.

"I am Saelithra."

She paused.

"And you carry the rot."

Thane blinked. Her eyes—if they were eyes—were fixed on him.

"And the thread," she added, voice softer now. "The world's wound and its stitch."

No one moved. Not even the wind dared stir.

Thane didn't reply. He wasn't sure he could. Her words had slid into him like needles, quiet and barbed.

Nerro stepped forward. He knelt, not in worship, not

fully. More like acknowledgment. Respect offered with caution. He reached into the satchel and drew out the crystalline vials. There were four. Each filled with a mist of light or shadow, each one softly humming in his hand.

He held them out to her.

"Memories," he said. "Freely given."

Saelithra approached without sound. Her veil of masks rippled—one flashed with greed, another with hunger, another with something unreadable. She didn't touch the vials right away. She circled them, head tilted, scenting them like a wolf. Then she hovered a finger over one that pulsed in gentle gold.

It was Thane's memory. He knew it even before Nerro flinched slightly, trying to warn her with a glance, but it was too late. She plucked it delicately from the tray, lifting it to her lips.

"Payment..." she murmured, breath catching. "Almost fair."

And she drank. Not quickly. Slowly. Like wine at a funeral. Like she didn't want the taste to end. Light flared across her skin, leaking through the masks, illuminating them from within. For a moment, it felt like spring had broken through her in full bloom. Then she stoppered the vial again—some of the gold liquid still inside—and let out a long, quiet sigh.

"Yes," she whispered. "This will do."

Her tongue ran slowly across her lips, savoring the last taste.

Thane's gut twisted. He didn't even remember what memory it was, but whatever it had been, it was clean and untouched. One of the only things he hadn't ruined. And now it belonged to her. Taken from him.

A wind moved. Not a breeze, just pressure, like something immense had exhaled. Saelithra turned and, without a word, began to walk. The forest bent with her passing. Branches lifted, moss peeled back, and roots shifted just enough to let her through.

They followed, matching her pace.

The glade narrowed to a path, winding through trees whose trunks shimmered with embedded crystal—amethyst veins pulsing softly, as if drawing breath. They descended, the light thinning with each step, until they reached a chamber that felt less like a place and more like the inside of something living.

A tree stood at its center, vast and ancient. Its roots had split the stone long ago, growing not just around but through a lattice of bone and metal and crystalline strands. Silver light leaked from fractures in its bark. The air smelled like burnt ozone and blooming lilac.

Saelithra raised a hand.

"You've come here for the truth. The path forward."

She stepped closer to the tree, but there was no reverence, just familiarity, as if it had always known her. She turned, her eyes fixed on Thane.

"When Arbelon still held breath and balance, there was one who came from your world. A man broken by illness, haunted by time. He came seeking answers—like you."

Her masks shifted—one showed sorrow, another pity. The third showed a flame burning out.

"But instead, he gave himself. Willingly. Not to death, but to balance. To life."

Thane frowned. Something twisted behind his ribs.

"He *became* the Heart."

The others stood frozen. Only the tree made sound, creaking slightly as its limbs swayed against a wind none of them felt.

"In that sacrifice, it was necessary that his soul be split," she continued, "one half grounded and bright—

purposeful and protective. The other—wild, unanchored, and afraid."

She looked at Thane.

"It is that half that escaped. The one you call Echo."

Something cold rippled through his spine.

"And now, the wound bleeds," she said. "And as long as it does… our worlds unravel."

Silence. Thick and endless followed. Then she spoke again.

"Arbelon. Faelenshara. And your Earth… they brush against one another—threads caught in the same loom. But only two bleed, only two share the burden."

She turned, her voice sharpening like frost on steel.

"And we are no fools. When the womb of the Heart fades, its children die. And the Fae will not die for Arbelon."

Her masks flared with finality.

"If the Heart cannot be repaired, we will sever the ties before that can ever happen."

Thane didn't move. Even if he'd wanted to, he couldn't. He stared at the tree. At the glowing lattice. At the quiet bones half-swallowed in bark. His father had done this, but not as escape. As sacrifice. Still, her words didn't stagger him. Instead, a quiet revelation slid beneath his skin, welcome and impossible to ignore.

He didn't speak it. Didn't even look at the others, but it held tight in his mind.

If my father came across somehow… if he escaped his fate… maybe I can too. And maybe she could come here too—his mother. Maybe we could be together, somewhere where I don't have to die.

This thought changed things completely.

Around him, the silence shifted—cracking at the edges, stretching under the weight of what had been said. The others stood scattered near the tree, a mixture of shock and betrayal, afraid to speak. Erynn's brow furrowed in concentration, and Lirien had gone still, eyes distant, her hands limp at her side, defeated.

But Thane felt energized, renewed. The Fae's revelation hadn't floored him, not outwardly, but something in his balance had tilted. Not just because his father had become the Heart and not just because the Echo was a piece of him, but because it made too much sense. Like it had always been true. Like part of him had known it from the beginning and just refused to admit it.

Saelithra watched him. Her masks moved slowly now, one dissolving into the next like clouds across the moon.

"You begin to see it, don't you?" she asked. "The thread between wound and healing. Between rot and root."

Thane's voice came rough, lower than he expected. "What do I do?"

Saelithra stepped lightly to the base of the tree. Her fingers brushed one of the crystal veins coiled through its roots. It pulsed once beneath her touch.

"You must mend what was broken," she said.

Her voice didn't rise. If anything, it softened, but the chamber seemed to shiver around it.

"The wild half of the Heart—the part unmoored—must return."

"You mean Echo," Thane said, the name bitter in his mouth.

"I mean the soul," she replied. "It must be guided. Drawn back into the lattice. The split must be undone."

Thane shook his head. "He's not just some broken puzzle piece. He's—he's chaos. He's *rage*. He's trying to tear this world apart."

Saelithra tilted her head.

"He is what remains when a sacrifice lives half-finished."

Her words felt surgical.

"He is grief without tether. Magic without name. But he is not beyond return."

She turned, slowly now, facing them all, but her gaze never really left Thane.

"To restore him to the Heart…" she said, "he must be rebound to it."

Lirien stirred. "That's impossible. Echo would never accept—"

"Wild Magic freely given," Saelithra said, cutting her off. "Not stolen. Not forced. Offered. Woven."

Thane's mouth went dry. "What the hell does that even mean?" he asked, his bitterness flaring back for a moment.

Saelithra stepped closer. Not looming—never looming—but impossibly present.

"Only a soul torn between worlds may stitch them again," she said. "Only one who has walked both realms—bled in both—can bridge what was broken." Her gaze pierced him like frost through bone. "It must be you."

The words landed like a verdict.

Thane's hands curled into fists. "No."

"Why not?" she asked.

"Because I didn't ask for this," he snapped. "Because I didn't sign up to be some god-damn needle in a loom of dying worlds."

The masks on her face shivered again, something like amusement, then something like pity. "And yet, here you are."

He didn't reply.

After a long pause, she added, almost gently. "Beware the thread, Thane. To weave the broken back together, the thread must pass through all wounds. Be sure you know which are yours."

The words echoed in the chamber like ripples on glass.

Thane turned away, jaw clenched. His stomach felt hollow. Somewhere behind him, Erynn whispered, "We must return to Felderwin. To Aelith."

Lirien didn't answer, but her silence said enough. Thane could feel it between them—something fragile and dividing. Not anger. Not yet, but certainty pulling in opposite directions.

He closed his eyes. The task was impossible, the cost unknowable, and yet, somehow, it still wasn't the worst part. The worst part was he knew it had to be done, and he was the only one who could do it.

Thane opened his eyes. The glade had gone still again, but not in reverence this time. In warning.

Then it happened.

A pulse. Small at first, barely visible, then a flicker of light from the face of Thane's watch. He glanced down just as the glow spread across his arm, veining through his skin like static lightning. It moved with a rhythm too steady to be random. Too slow to be natural. A heartbeat made of static. The hairs on his neck rose.

Saelithra's expression shifted. But this time it wasn't with intrigue or subtle control. No, this time it was fear, clear and unbridled.

"You brought that here?" she whispered. The masks across her face rippled—then stilled, frozen in something that looked too much like terror.

Nerro turned, saw the glow on Thane's wrist, and gasped.

All at once, the chamber changed. The silver branches overhead quivered. The crystals in the roots began to pulse, faint but synchronous, echoing the beat of Thane's arm. Shadows deepened in unnatural ways, climbing instead of falling, smearing instead of stretching.

Thane staggered a step backward. "I didn't—what are you talking about?"

Saelithra stepped toward him, her movement sharp, all grace gone. "Do you even know what you carry?" she hissed. Her masks rippled through grief, rage, horror—too fast to track. She wasn't looking at Thane anymore. She was looking at the thing connected to him.

"It's just a watch," Thane said, but even he didn't believe it or understand what it was.

"It is a tether," she said, her voice suddenly low. "And through it, he reaches."

The glade itself seemed to recoil. Trees flickered—literally. For an instant, their branches snapped into pixelated shards before smoothing back. Leaves glitched midair and the air warped like water.

Nerro stepped forward, urgent. "My lady—"

She spun to him. "Go. Tell the others. The Wyrdwall must be raised."

He didn't argue. He turned and vanished into the trees.

"The Wyrdwall?" Lirien asked, already reaching for her blade.

"It's a Fae warding," Erynn answered, eyes wide. "Veils. Illusions. Confusion spells. Meant to cloak and confuse and protect."

Saelithra turned to Thane again.

"Do you not feel it? The pull? You've bound yourself to him, to a rift—and it pulls both ways."

Thane's hand curled at his side. "Why now?" he asked. "Why is it doing this?"

"Because you're connected to him," she said. "Because you've taken the first stitch in the loom. And now he sees the thread."

Then a voice echoed out from nowhere and everywhere, like a loudspeaker, coiled and sharp and full of rot. It crawled through the air, tight as wire, soaked in hate.

"You would unmake me?" Echo said. "Then see what it will cost you, Saelithra."

Thane dropped to one knee, clutching his skull as a fresh pulse blasted through the watch. The glow flared, then darkened. The air split, and behind him, the glade *tore*. Reality buckled, and a seam opened. Not with thunder or quake, but with silence. A terrible silence. The kind that didn't belong to this world or any other.

The air behind Thane sheared sideways, folding in on itself like torn silk, glitching through dimensions. Colors bled from the world. Sounds flattened. Light staggered.

Then a shape, massive, grotesque, and impossible. It didn't walk so much as emerge—claw first, then forelimb, then a maw lined in luminous thorns. A creature of bone and bloom, draped in dying petals, teeth like knives carved from pearl. Its skin moved like a slow wave of petals and hunger. A Fae-Eater. A myth, from stories whispered in Falensharan twilight.

Now, it stepped through, and the glade recoiled. Trees withered in its presence. Crystal roots cracked. The air shuddered with impossible pressure.

Saelithra turned—not to flee, not to cower, but to *command*. She raised both arms, her voice like thunder channeled through a hymn.

"Raise the Wyrdwall!"

And from the edge of the glade, it began to form. The Wyrdwall shimmered to life with threads of light and illusion and song spiraling upward in a web of spectral flame. A great ring of protection—Fae magic woven ancient and deep—began knitting itself around the grove.

But it was too late. The Fae-Eater had already breached. Its leg drove into the glade, twisting the ground beneath it, reality folding like wet paper. Where it stepped, nothing grew. Where it breathed, color bled out of leaves. Faelings near the edge of the clearing shrieked and vanished, unable to hold their form in its presence.

Saelithra's expression hardened. No masks now, only her. "You must leave," she said to Thane. But her voice did not ask, it boomed, it commanded.

"NOW."

She turned to the crystalline tree, without ceremony or blessing. Just raw force with a motion like tearing silk, and a glyph seared into her palm as she opened a second rift. Not clean or sacred, but violent and unchecked.

The rift ripped sideways behind Thane, the edges lined in blood-light and fraying code, threads of raw Fae magic screaming between. The suction hit like gravity inverted, and Thane's feet left the ground. The rift pulled at him, sucking him through. His limbs flailed. Vision fractured, and the last thing he saw—just before the rift snapped shut —was the Fae descending. Dozens of them. Hundreds, maybe. It didn't matter. They were falling upon the beast, chanting in ancient tongue, vanishing and reappearing as they struck like blades of light and thorn.

And the creature? It laughed.

Then nothing.

No sound. No color. No sense of anything.

Only the pull—like being yanked through an airlock into the cold between stars.

Only the darkness. Infinite and collapsing at the same time.

And in it, Thane did not feel fear and there was no pain.

Only one thought remained. Looping. Quiet. Unbreakable.

I have to save him.

1 3

<hr>

ONLY HER VOICE

Thane came back wrong.

There was no slow fade, no gentle transition, only light, heat, and the sound of something crackling beside his skull. He gasped and nearly toppled out of the chair, head lolling sideways as sweat rolled down the bridge of his nose. His skin was clammy, and his shirt was soaked. The room spun around him in dizzy arcs.

Then came the smell—burnt circuitry, sharp and acrid, already thick in the air.

His vision wobbled into clarity just in time to see the VR headset still glowing faintly, one side of it sparking with little hisses of dying heat. The frame was cracked. Plastic warped where Saelithra had...

Saelithra.

Her image lingered in the backs of his eyes. Not her voice, only her image. Half-loaded. Half-rendered. Like the scene stuttered mid-frame, pulling her face apart behind warped glass. Her features floated in shards, unfinished. Her mouth moved but said nothing.

Then more sparks. One final pop of resistance. Then

the screen blinked dark, and the circle on the headset flashed red—the red ring of death. Faint at first, then steady and glaring.

He ripped the thing from his head and stared at it in horror. It was hot, burned in places, and one of the straps had melted where the casing had split. A fine crack ran across the top curve of the display as a whisper of black smoke curled from the lower vent.

This wasn't like the other times. This felt… directed. It was like something had kicked him out, spitting him back into a body that didn't quite fit. He swallowed hard. His hands were already moving, checking for heat damage, assessing what could be salvaged because one thing was clear, he needed it working again.

He cleared the desk with a sweep of his arm—notes, wrappers, an empty pill bottle scattering to the floor. The headset hit the desk like a corpse. He dove in without any hesitation, grabbed his tools from the drawer.

The casing came off with a sharp crack. Heat rolled out, nearly burning his palm. A scorched capacitor had fused to its socket, and a line of wiring had melted straight through the plastic ridge. He exhaled hard and grabbed a donor board from an old graphics card in the bin beside the bed. He pressed on, working blind, muscle memory taking over where reason fell short. Tiny screws. Fragile solder points. Copper lines like veins.

Sweat trickled down his spine.

The smell was worse now—sickly, metallic. He clipped a scorched connector and replaced it with a rigged bypass. Swapped a blown chip with one from his father's old toolkit. Re-routed the power relay through the stabilizer core. The thing was a Frankenstein mess. Nothing in it matched anymore.

It pulsed once, still red. He held his breath.

Again—red.

But then it morphed to… blue. A faint hum. The ring blinked once, then steadied. The fractured startup logo—the broken circle—shimmered across the display.

He slumped back in his chair. A breath of relief catching in his chest before it could leave his mouth.

Then a voice called from down the hall.

"Dinner's ready!"

He flinched so hard, the headset slipped from his fingers and clattered to the desk. For a heartbeat, the voice felt like hers—Saelithra's. Same cadence. Same edge of urgency. But the voice from the hall wasn't from Arbelon. It was from here, on Earth. Footsteps padded down the hall, and Thane scrambled to shove the headset into a drawer just as his mother reached the door.

Her footsteps paused there, waiting, but she didn't come in and rapped her knuckle on the door instead.

"Come eat," she called again, softer this time. "It's getting cold."

Thane didn't answer, but his hands were still shaking as he turned grabbing his cane and plodding across the room.

A moment later, he stepped into the kitchen and stopped cold. The light was too bright and clean. It cast long shapes over linoleum tiles and stainless steel, stopping just short of the table. A woman stood at the stove, back turned, humming softly to herself as she stirred something steaming in a pot. The scent of garlic and tomato filled the room. Comfort food.

She was talking again, something about his appetite, about how he needed to eat more, about how the pasta would be ready in just a second.

She knew him. That much was obvious, but then she turned, and her face—it wasn't gone. It was there. All the features accounted for: eyes, nose, mouth. She smiled at him, but to Thane it was static. Blurred. Like a video feed that wouldn't buffer, playing just out of focus. His brain reached for recognition, but there was nothing to grab onto. There was no connection or anchor, only noise. He knew he was supposed to know her. Every part of him screamed that, but she was a stranger.

Then she spoke again.

"Sit down, baby. You look pale."

And that's when he knew.

The voice. Not the face. The voice.

Warm, frayed at the edges. Worn into the corners of his memories like an old record. That voice had once read him bedtime stories, whispered lullabies, scolded him when he'd lied about brushing his teeth. It was her. It had always been her.

His mother.

He clung to the sound of her voice like a lifeline.

She smiled again—wider this time—and slid a plate across the counter toward him.

"You okay?" she asked.

Thane nodded, barely.

"Yeah," he lied. "I'm just tired."

She turned back to the stove, humming again, lifting a glass salt shaker from beside the burner. The small crystal one, shaped like a teardrop. She turned it in her fingers, letting the light catch along its faceted sides.

Thane froze. A memory surfaced—unbidden, immediate.

That shaker. The same shimmer. The same turn of the wrist. He'd seen it before, but not here. Not in this kitchen. It looked just like the memory vial. The one Nerro had deposited the memory drawn from his mind into. The one he had handed to Saelithra like a gift. The one Saelithra had drank, slowly and deliberately, savoring each drop.

He blinked hard and his stomach clenched. It wasn't just a borrowed memory. It was the trade. The memory he gave to cross the threshold into Faelenshara, but now he knew they'd taken more because he at least knew her face shouldn't have gone with it. The shape of her smile, the laugh lines near her eyes were gone, all just static now. Erased from his mind.

He stared at the side of her face, trying to reassemble it in his mind. Pull it back into focus.

But nothing came.

Just that salt shaker and her voice.

He squeezed his eyes shut. Hard. Hoping the pressure might summon the image back, but all he got was noise. Hissing, indistinct, and unformed.

He should remember. He *wanted* to remember. But instead, the anger bloomed—quiet at first, like heat behind his ears. Then spreading. Frustration bleeding into fear.

He clenched his fists beneath the table.

Why couldn't he see her?

Why couldn't he see the one thing that mattered in this place?

His mother didn't look up at first. She stirred the sauce, humming softly, then reached for the pan of bread in the oven. A practiced rhythm, that much was familiar, but Thane couldn't take his eyes off her—studying her. Quiet. Something about it was… wrong. Not wrong exactly— just *off*, like some heavy weight filled the distance between them.

She set the bread on the stovetop and finally glanced over. Their eyes didn't quite meet, and her smile faltered for just a second.

"You've been quiet lately," she said. "You feeling a little… off?"

Thane didn't answer.

He could see the concern forming behind her eyes—

the questions, the calculation. She was trying to be gentle, but there was something beneath her tone. Something afraid, and he knew that look. It was the same one she used to wear around the time his dad got sick. Really sick.

She sat down across from him, wiping her hands on a towel. "Do you remember much, you know, from when your dad was… fading?" she asked, voice careful.

He tensed, jaw tight. "Some."

Her eyes searched his face. "He used to talk about places. After the diagnosis. Places that didn't exist."

She looked down at the table, rubbing a thumb across a knot in the wood.

"There were stories he'd tell again and again. He said there was a valley of cliffs, with a city wedged between them. Towers like spindles—made of something like glass, only it looked like oil on water. And a lake that shimmered… with memories, he said. Memories of the lost. The fallen. I'd sit and listen. Just humoring him. I thought…"

She paused, wiping a tear from her eye before glancing up at him.

"His dementia was a lot to handle."

The silence that followed wasn't heavy. It was hollow, like a room missing furniture that should have been there.

Thane exhaled through his nose, and his pulse throbbed behind his eyes. The silence stretched, not because he didn't know what to say, but because he *did*, and saying it would make it real.

He looked up.

"That wasn't dementia, Mom."

Her head tilted, just slightly. "Honey—"

"I've been there." His voice was flat and hollow. "I saw him."

She blinked once and froze.

"He's still there," Thane continued, slower now. "In Arbelon. He's… part of it."

She didn't speak. Didn't move an inch.

He pressed on. "There's this thing—the Heart—it's like a source of magic, or memory, or maybe both. It's connected to everything. To *him*. He's not dead, not really. He *became* something, and I've seen it. Felt it. I know it sounds—"

"Please don't," she whispered, cutting through him. Her eyes were glassy. "Please don't sound like him."

Jane didn't wait for him to respond. She stood and turned away, her shoulders hunched as she leaned into the counter. Quiet at first. Just breathing. But her hands gripped the edge so tightly, her knuckles whitened.

"I lost him," she said, barely audible. "To something I couldn't fight. He stopped eating. Stopped sleeping. Stopped *being here*. Day by day, he slipped somewhere I couldn't follow."

She shook her head, the motion jerky.

"Don't make me lose you too."

Thane sat there, hollowed out, but he still responded. She was all he had left in this place. "You haven't," he said softly. "I'm right here."

She turned to face him. Tears streaked her cheeks. Her smile quivered as she reached down and touched his face —gently, as if afraid her hand might pass through.

"And I'm right here too," she said.

But Thane couldn't see her. Not really. Not the details —the shape of her face, the pursing of her lips, the lock of hair that fell across her eyes. None of it, just the voice, the outline. Her hand was warm on his skin, but her face was nothing but static. A blur, like a ghost of something he once knew. He blinked again, trying to fix it, but it was gone. Whatever he'd lost—whatever *they'd* taken—wasn't coming back.

Thane didn't say anything more. He'd already said too much.

She stood there—eyes wet, smile trembling—still trying to hold on to the idea that he could be saved. That he wasn't already halfway gone.

He didn't have the heart to press her. *Later,* he told himself. *Next time.*

He stepped back from the table, whispered that he was tired, and kissed her cheek before slipping away down the hall. The walk back to his room felt longer than it should've. He moved like a shadow, like someone afraid of waking a world that had already started to forget him.

Inside his room, the light from the desk lamp still glowed. The drawer was still open. The headset waited, silent, cracked, and repaired, but barely.

Thane sat down. His hand hovered over the thing, fingers brushing the plastic shell. He didn't feel afraid. Not this time. If anything, he was more certain than ever. Arbelon was real. The Heart was real. His father hadn't been crazy, and neither was he.

This world—Earth—had already started letting go.

But Arbelon… that one still remembered him.

He took a breath. Slipped the headset on, and clicked the button.

There was a flicker… then static… then darkness. A silence that didn't belong to Earth.

A whisper like memory.

And somewhere, far away, something began to pull him home.

14

STITCHED TOGETHER

THANE SURFACED WITHOUT SOUND.

One breath he was on Earth—dim lamp light, carpeted floors, the fading memory of his mother's voice— and the next, he was here.

Not gasp or any signs of disorientation this time. He arrived with a stillness so unnatural it felt like waking into someone else's dream. Cold air kissed his face as his body sank slightly into damp moss. The steady hush of the waterfall filled his ears.

Thane opened his eyes. Mist clung to the tree-line, soft and unmoving, and the waterfall spilled down into its wide basin just beyond. The air smelled of stone and moss. But something was missing. The stone cottage that had sat beside the pool was gone. And there was no sign of Orren crouched by the pool. It was only the rocks and the falls and the sky above them, as the daylight was darkening into evening.

Behind him, the others were stirring. Rising at the same moment he had, as if pulled up by the same invisible thread. Erynn to his left, Kaelir kneeling, shaking his head clear. Lirien, already on her feet, silent and scanning.

The air felt heavy, charged with a kind of quiet that didn't belong—not serene, not peaceful. More unsettling and off.

He was trying to piece it together. The last he recalled, they'd been in the thick of it, and then they'd simply been *removed*—as if Saelithra had merely blinked and sent them all out of Faelenshara. They weren't given a choice. They were asked their opinion. It just happened.

Thane sat up. His hands were steady. There was no blood this time, and no throbbing behind his eyes. The last few jumps to Earth and back had torn at him, made his skin stretch, made the world pulse like bad code. But this time… nothing.

He touched the inside of his nose and then his ear anyway. Dry.

It was wrong. It was just too clean and too damn easy.

And behind him, the falls flowed on as if none of it had happened. But it had.

His mother's voice stuck with him, but the old memories of her face were gone—replaced now by fresh ones. He recalled everything she'd said about his father. About his stories of Arbelon. He'd tried to tell her the truth—about the Heart, about his father's sacrifice to save a world. That he might still be alive.

Kaelir finally rose. "Where's the stone cottage? And Orren?"

"It was right there," Erynn murmured, rising next to her brother, turning in a slow circle. "I swear it was—"

"It's gone," Lirien said. "So is Orren." Her tone didn't invite argument.

Thane stayed silent. His thoughts were moving slower than usual. They weren't sluggish, he was just trying to square up everything that his mother had just shared with the words from Saelithra, and struggling to make sense of it all.

"Was it real?" Erynn asked, turning to Kaelir. Her voice weak. "Orren, Nerro, Saelithra? Faelenshara?"

No one answered. They all stood in silence. Everyone taking in their own version of this new reality.

Thane stared at the spot where Orren's cottage had been. He didn't trust how easily they'd been returned. He didn't trust how muddled his thoughts were, and he definitely didn't trust the way *Arbelon* seemed to be inviting him to stay. But one thing was certain. It had happened. All of it. And it wasn't over.

"It was all real," Thane said.

No one acknowledged his words, but they all turned—just a little. Just enough to show they'd been thinking the same.

Kaelir moved to the edge of the pool. His reflection stretched across the water, long, lean, and wavering. "That thing we saw…" Kaelir said, then frowned. "What *was* it?"

Lirien turned at the question. "It was a Fae-Eater, a thing of myth and mystery."

Erynn cleared her throat. "It wasn't just a Fae-Eater," she said quietly. She was standing now, arms at her sides, gaze far away. "That was the Kerridax."

The name itself seemed to settle on the glade like a second silence.

"A creature of exile," she went on, "and unmaking. A myth so old and dangerous, even the Fae speak of it in hushed tones. It unthreads what doesn't belong—gate walkers, dreamers, destroyers… even the Fae themselves."

She paused, then added, almost to herself, "The Kerridax awakens only when the veil thins… In every age, it finds a way to feed, and it seems they answer to Echo now."

The quiet that followed didn't feel empty. It felt occupied and futile. They didn't move for a moment longer. They just stood there, four broken silhouettes in the dimming light, each haunted by something they weren't ready to name.

Thane spoke first. He didn't recount everything—not what the Fae had stolen from him or the way his mother looked at him like she knew he was already half gone—but he told them what mattered. "I saw my father in the Heart before..." he said, his voice trailing, eyes fixed on the waterfall. "And we all heard it from Saelithra, Echo is what broke off, and now it wants to break everything else."

He let the words sit for a moment.

"I tried to tell my mother. I tried to explain, but she didn't believe me. Still, I think... I think she knew more than she said."

Lirien crossed her arms tightly, jaw set. Her eyes didn't leave Thane.

"That thing—Echo—it didn't like what Saelithra shared." Thane said. "It *raged*. Not out loud. But I felt it— like something clawing at the inside of my skull."

Erynn looked down at his watch. The second hand slid from tick to tick behind the faceplate. Not pausing. "Do you think... he's listening again now?" she asked.

Kaelir shifted backward. Lirien's eyes narrowed, but Thane didn't flinch. "It's fine. I understand the connection now. I can feel it..." he paused. "And I can make it stop." But he didn't explain *how* he did that, and no one pushed him.

Kaelir glanced toward the far edge of the pool—the place where the portal had opened to Faelensahra, where they'd walked in with Nerro.

Nothing remained of the gateway. There was no shimmer, no rift. Nothing but the sound of the falls and a wind that rippled across the water.

"She said 'now.' Not later," Erynn murmured, eyes fixed on the empty space.

Kaelir nodded slowly. "Then we finish it. We complete what needs to be done." He said it like a command, but it didn't carry weight, only weariness.

They stood in silence a moment longer. Then Lirien turned without a word and started toward the trees.

"Where are you going?" Erynn asked.

"Whatever needs to be done. Wherever we need to go. It's not here. We need to return to Swain, to our boat," she said without turning. "We're wasting time. Devendor waits. *He* waits."

Erynn stepped after her. "We should return to Felderwin. We don't know what we're heading into. Not really. We should regroup, speak to Aelith and Thassriel—"

"We've already spoken to them," Lirien cut in. "We have Thane. He is all we need to get this done, and the less who know our task, the better."

"But we need a plan," Kaelir said, trying to steady the moment. "One cannot just walk into Devendor. We need allies and resources. Not just dreams and riddles."

Lirien stopped, her back to them. "Then stay. Draw your maps. Draft your plans. But the Heart won't wait. You heard her just as I did. Our worlds are fading, and the Fae intend to sacrifice Arbelon to save their own."

The silence that followed stretched. Not sharp—just long.

Everyone turned to Thane, but he didn't move.

"We don't even know if we *can* get back in," he said finally. "To the Heart or even find Echo."

He didn't say it to provoke. He just said it, and somehow, it was the worst thing yet—because it was true. No one responded. There were neither agreements nor protest, only a long breath that didn't belong to any of them.

A splinter formed—not loud, not jagged. But real, and from that point forward, none of them looked at each other the same.

Lirien stepped forward, toward Swain, and the others followed.

They followed the stream. It wound out from the waterfall's basin, narrow and fast-moving. White foam coating its surface. The sun was low on the horizon, leaving the trees painted in long shadows that moved even when the wind didn't.

Branches creaked above them. The ground sloped downward in shallow steps, and moss clung to the rocks like peeling skin. The farther they walked, the stranger the terrain became.

The grass lost its texture. Not all at once, but gradually. Blades once sharp and fine now blurred at the edges, as if rendered by an artist in a hurry. Thane brushed his fingers through them, and the sensation was there, cool and damp, but it didn't linger. No scent. No residue. It was like touching something that wasn't fully convinced of being real.

They all could see the strangeness, but the silence held tight. Swain was falling further into the veil, or somewhere beyond this world.

Ahead, the trees shifted. One moment a trunk stood solid and firm, either an oak or elm, hard to tell. Then, when Thane looked away and back again, it had become two trunks, slightly farther apart, their limbs bending in new directions.

Again, no one said a word. But they walked slower. Warier.

Lirien was first to glance at the horizon. She stopped walking. The others followed her gaze. The sky flickered. Just once. A stutter, like a frame skipping in a broken film reel. The ridge-line beyond the trees rippled faintly, its outline fuzzing for half a breath before resolving.

"Did you see that?" Kaelir muttered, low.

Erynn nodded. "We need to move through this place, fast. It's falling apart."

There were murmurs of acknowledgment, and when they set off again, the pace was brisk with a renewed purpose.

The stream grew quieter, and the trees thinned. The air felt thinner, too, like it wasn't pressing down the way it should. Sounds carried too far in places, nowhere in others.

Swain was close now. But Arbelon was already changing around them, and not one of them dared ask if Thane was causing it. They already knew.

The closer they moved to Swain, things continued to twist and bend. A flicker. Then the stream appeared beneath Erynn's feet.

She gasped and stumbled, landing hard on one knee. Water soaked her boots, but there was no water beneath her. Only moss and stone. Then the stream blinked back into place, as if it had never left its banks.

Kaelir caught her arm, hauling her upright. "I've seen battlefields less twisted," he muttered. "This is not good."

No one disagreed.

The trees around them no longer waited to be noticed. Now they bent in impossible angles, their limbs reversed, and shadows cast without sources. One tree split in two like a forked path mid-blink. Another shed its bark in a loop, like a rewinding reel no one could pause.

The further they walked, the more the world glitched.

"It's like we're walking through a corrupted dream," Lirien whispered. Her voice sounded too loud. Then too quiet. Then not at all.

Thane didn't answer. He was mesmerized by what he was seeing. He was watching Kaelir's outline flicker. Just slightly. Like a rendering delay catching up to a moving model. Then Erynn's cheek glitched, half a breath out of sync with her jawline before snapping back. Lirien's hair looped for a heartbeat as she stepped forward. Even their voices were falling out of step.

It wasn't violent. Not yet. Just… wrong. But he said nothing. Because if he said it out loud, it became real. And if it became real, it might never go away. So he walked, pretending not to notice, and the others did the same, but they all felt it now: they weren't walking through Arbelon anymore—they were walking through something pretending to be.

The path narrowed. Not by terrain, but by… distortion. Trees crowded in, then blurred apart. Ground dipped where it hadn't a moment ago. The stream veered sharply west—then didn't.

And then they saw them. Figures. Just ahead. Maybe six. Maybe twenty. All distant. All still. Villagers, by the look of them—at least from afar. Loose tunics. Simple trousers. Pale faces blurred by mist.

The group slowed.

"Something's wrong," Kaelir muttered, hand drifting to the hilt of his blade.

"Just keep moving," Lirien said, flat.

But they all hesitated. The villagers were facing them, but not with *their* faces. One had its head cocked sideways at an impossible angle, eyes pointing toward the ground, feet marching toward them anyway. Another stood with one leg rooted into the path like a tree stump, the other jerking forward every few seconds, dragging the torso behind like it didn't know how to walk.

"Stay close," Kaelir said.

They stepped off the trail. Edged closer. That's when they saw the stitching. Not metaphorical. Not poetic. Real stitches. Thick, crude thread. Sewn through arms and shoulders and necks. Flesh joined to bark. Human limbs fused with branches and scales and fur. One had a torso far too small for its head, and its head was wrong—childlike on one side, feline on the other, both mouths slightly open as if caught between gasps.

And then one turned. Not smoothly. Not all at once. But just parts of it. Its mouth didn't open, but they heard the voice anyway.

"Welcome to Swain… welcome to Swain… welcome to Swain…"

It repeated like a wind-up box with a cracked gear.

Another villager joined it. Then another. All different. All grotesque. Each one stitched from pieces that didn't belong together.

"Back away," Kaelir said under his breath, sword now in hand.

"Too late," Erynn whispered. "They've seen us."

But the stitched things didn't move to attack. They just stood there. Glitching. Looping. Chanting.

Swain had found them, but it was not a place anymore. It was a festering wound. A tear in the world's fabric.

Erynn pulled Thane back by the arm, harder than she meant to. "We're *not* going into that," she hissed.

Thane didn't argue. None of them did.

Lirien's face had gone pale. Not with fear, but from

something deeper. Recognition or disgust, maybe both. "I've never…" she said, her voice trailing off.

Kaelir stared at the stitched things, still looping their chant in a broken chorus. "The whole place is rotten," he muttered. "We can't go through."

Thane glanced back toward the warped villagers. They hadn't moved, but one—its limbs staggered in uneven proportions—lifted a hand in slow, segmented motion. Not a wave. Not a threat. Just… acknowledgment, like it *knew* him.

"We follow the river," Kaelir said. "Not toward Swain. The other way. Upstream."

Lirien nodded. Erynn hesitated, but didn't argue. They turned without another word. The sound of the stitched things followed them for a while.

"Welcome to Swain… welcome to Swain…"

The chant distorted—slowed—then faded entirely. But the unease didn't. They retraced their steps and passed the waterfall without speaking. No one looked back. The pool, the stitched things, the chants, none of it followed, but it stayed with them anyway.

The path rose steadily as they moved along the stream above the falls, winding through the lower foothills. Here, the terrain grew harsher. Rocks jutted like old teeth from the soil. Chaparral spread in golden tufts between them, brittle and sharp. A few scattered trees clung to the slopes, their limbs bent and wind-stripped. The land offered no shelter, no welcome—only exposure, and they felt it. All of them.

Kaelir paused once to scan the horizon, but Lirien didn't wait. She walked ahead alone, a slim silhouette against the twilight, the silvery tendrils of moonlight casting just enough light to stay on track.

Kaelir fell behind, lingering near the rear. Watching and calculating.

Erynn walked near Thane, but said nothing. Just a glance now and then. Not accusing, but also not trusting. Waiting, maybe—for him to speak. To choose. To lead.

But he didn't because the silence had weight to it. Whatever unity they'd carried from Felderwin, whatever clarity they'd grasped beyond the waterfall… he could feel it slipping. The glitches had stopped. That should've helped, but it didn't. It only made the silence louder.

Thane adjusted the strap on his shoulders, gaze fixed ahead. His legs moved without thought. His body following the path on muscle memory. But his mind had drifted— fractured, like the group behind him. Torn between Felderwin and Devendor. Uncertain which path to take.

And in that silence, the voice returned. Soft. Just behind his ear.

"You could bring her here. Your mother."

He froze. Just half a step. Looking down, his watch pulsed with a subtle glow. He quickly covered with his sleeve, glancing at the others, but no one had noticed.

Then Echo again.

"I could show you how."

Thane didn't answer. Not even in his thoughts.

He clenched his jaw, exhaled slow, and kept walking. But the voice lingered. Not mocking. Not cruel. Just… patient.

As if it already knew what he wanted.

And who he'd betray to get it.

15

WINGS IN THE ASH

The fire at their camp had long gone cold. They sat in a half-circle of stone and shadow beneath the shoulder of a ruined hill, the stars smeared behind drifting smoke. No one spoke, not at first, but the silence had teeth.

The foothills north of Swain felt emptier now. But it wasn't just quiet, it was hollow, as if the land itself had flinched from whatever they'd stirred in Faelenshara. Charred scrub stretched across the slope, and the trees here leaned like dying things, their bark bleached, branches curled inward.

Thane sat apart. Not far, just… apart. His back was resting against a boulder gone slick with moss. He lifted his head, watching the others, watching the flicker of motion as Erynn shifted her weight or Kaelir ran an oil cloth on his blade. Lirien crouched near the edge of the slope, arms on her knees, her face turned to the dark horizon.

Eventually, Erynn broke the quiet. Her voice was steady, but dry.

"I know we've gone back and forth. But I really think we should head back to Felderwin."

Kaelir gave a short nod, confirming he'd already made the same decision himself. "We regroup. Warn the others, and prepare for what's to come."

"We don't have time." Thane didn't raise his voice, but it cut through just the same, weary and tired, but resolute.

Erynn turned her head, and Kaelir paused his work, looking up sharply.

Thane kept going. "You all heard it in Faelenshara. You heard it in Saelithra's voice, and saw the fear in her eyes, just as I did. She sent us away for a reason. If we wait—if we let Echo settle or regroup—we lose any advantage. We lose everything."

"Let's not forget, she is Fae, and their Queen at that," Erynn said. "Half-truths and hidden agendas. That's their way of life."

"Doesn't change the reality." Thane met her gaze. "I know what I heard, what I saw… and Swain." He shook his head, regathering his thoughts. "This place is breaking. And half of the Heart? That cannot sustain this world. Even I can see that."

"You think you know more than us?" Erynn asked, her temper flaring, uncharacteristic and raw.

Thane said nothing more, but he didn't turn away.

Kaelir rose to his feet. Slowly.

"You weren't here," he said, the muscles in his face taut as he tried to restrain his anger. "You saw none of it. You were lucky… you died, or left us—whatever you did. But we remained, living in your wreckage."

Lirien's voice came quiet from the edge. "Thane's right. Swain is already cracking, foretelling what is to come. We all saw it—none of this world is stable anymore. The Heart is failing. We all know it."

"Then that's all the more reason to move carefully," Erynn snapped, standing now. Her hand hovered near her belt, fingers twitching—not for a blade, but from the weight of the words. "We've lost too much already to gamble again on hunches and instincts."

Thane stood too. Slowly.

"I'm not asking you to gamble. I'm telling you what I saw. What I heard. That's all."

Erynn stepped forward. "And now… now you think you know better than us too?"

"No." Thane answered, his voice stayed low. "But I know what I am. And I know we don't get another chance."

Kaelir stepped between them, jaw tight. "You don't get to make this call on your own."

"You're right," Thane said. "I don't. But I can make it for *me*."

The air between them stilled, like the land being consumed by a lava flow. Kaelir's face twisted—not in rage, but something sharper. Something near betrayal.

He turned, spat, then looked back.

"Go," he said. "Do whatever you want. We were doing fine without you."

Thane didn't blink. "Yeah. It looks like it."

The words landed harder than either of them expected. Erynn's face fell. Lirien didn't turn. Kaelir about to step closer.

But then a sound like distant thunder rang out from the darkness. The ground rumbled beneath their feet, steady and deliberate, and growing louder.

The rumble deepened.

Lirien spoke the words everyone was thinking first. "That's not thunder."

The ground shook again—growing stronger, rhythmic and measured. Then came the shriek of a warhorn. Metal striking stone. A dozen hooves. A scream on the wind and the next moment the tree-line exploded.

Riders tore through it—black-armored, faceless, eyes burning with cold blue light. Hooves churned the ash-strewn soil. Behind them, things followed: not men, not beast. They were twisted silhouettes stitched from sinew and shell, their limbs bending wrong, crawling with the same viridian static that shimmered in the riders' wake.

Kaelir swore and moved before thought. He yanked Erynn behind him, his blade in hand. Erynn stumbled, caught herself, and then stood firm beside the others. But there was no line to be made, only the four of them standing against an onslaught.

The Riders weren't just charging, they were closing ranks. The cool blue of their eyes never fading. A shadow vaulted from one of the corrupted beasts, slamming into the rocks just feet from Thane, and he fell back, his breath knocked from his chest.

Next to him, the thing rose—six limbs and no face. Just a knot of teeth and hair and too many fingers twitching where its ribs should've been. Thane rolled as the creature lunged, a smear of wet breath cutting the air where his throat had been.

Kaelir's sword whistled past a beat later, cleaving the thing sideways.

"Move!" Kaelir barked.

Erynn's voice cracked across the hillside, but no one heard her. Not fully. The clash of metal and roar of broken creatures swallowed everything.

Then came a shriek that pierced the chaos. But this time it wasn't a warhorn or a voice. It was something ancient, descending out of the darkness.

A shadow tore overhead, cutting through the sky like a blade. Then another. And another.

Draconic shapes burst through the faint starlight, their wings wide and dark, clawed feet scattering ash and twisted bodies. Veilborn riders crouched low on their backs, their helms carved with ancient runes, their eyes hidden in shadow.

Lirien looked up, gasping—not in fear, but disbelief.

The Riders and their horses faltered for the first time. Their lines staggered as the air cracked with lightning and wind, the pressure of wingbeats knocking them sideways.

Thane stumbled, eyes tracking the lead drake as it banked low across the hillside, curling smoke in its wake before it landed mere yards away. The Veilborn leapt down, sword in hand. Then came his voice—half shout, half grin.

"Hey, outlander. You need some help?"

It was Bostick. Alive. He was clad in Veilborn armor, and wearing a crooked, impossible grin that stood out even in the chaos.

Kaelir turned toward the voice, eyes wide with something unspoken. First Rage, then recognition, and rounded out by relief. All braided together.

"I thought you were dead," Kaelir muttered, slamming his sword into the chest of a corrupted hound before stepping back-to-back with Bostick.

"Yeah, well…" Bostick parried a blow and grunted. "I'm stubborn like that. You, of anyone, should know that."

Together, they fought on.

Veilborn drakes swooped low, strafing the hillside with flame and fury. The Riders of the Ring regrouped, their numbers swelling as more dark shapes were still cresting the hillside like a rising tide.

And that tide should've turned, but the Riders of the Ring were no longer mortal things. Not anymore. They didn't bleed like men, and they didn't break like beasts. They moved with purpose—and that purpose was to capture Thane—at all costs.

As the Veilborn pressed forward and the drakes unleashed their flame, a cluster of black-armored Riders veered from the battle's heart. Four of them, jagged in silhouette and humming with viridian static, broke from the ranks, stepping toward Thane with terrifying precision.

He stepped back, unsure. His fingers twitched with instinct, and he reached for the magic, but he didn't move.

Erynn saw it first.

"No!" she shouted, and ran.

Kaelir spun, too slow to stop her.

Erynn surged forward with a scream, slamming her full weight into the nearest Rider. The strike was well-placed, her foot slamming into the joint of the Rider's knee, and he went down with a sickening crack.

The creature howled, but there was another just behind.

The second Rider pivoted by her side, silent and cruel, and drove a hooked blade across her midsection in a blur of black metal.

Steel met flesh.

For a moment, nothing moved. Not the Riders. Not Thane. Not the wind.

And then time broke.

Erynn's feet staggered. Her mouth opened, but no sound came—just a gasp as red bloomed across her tunic.

She dropped to her knees.

Kaelir's scream cracked the air—raw, wounded, and feral. He threw himself forward, carving into the Rider that felled her, blade meeting bone with a furious clash.

Thane bolted to Erynn's side, kneeling beside her.

His hands pressed against the wound, trying to stop the

bleeding. He reached for his magic—instinct and reflex—and it responded, filling his body with a surge so chaotic his breath caught. He grabbed on to the threads, pulling them tight as luminescent blue cracks rippled across his skin.

And then… moss sprouted from the stones, coating the ground beneath him, blooming outward from his knees like he'd seeded the earth with grief.

The Riders pressed closer. Their focus unshaken. Their steps in rhythm, always toward him.

From behind, Lirien's hand seized his arm.

"There's no time," Lirien hissed, her voice breaking. "If we are to see this world mended… then we have to go. Now."

Thane looked down at Erynn.

Her lips were moving, but no sound reached him—not over the battle. Just a faint tremor at the edges of her mouth, like she was trying to say something he already knew.

He pressed harder against the wound. More moss unfurled beneath him, crawling in uneven spirals. His magic flared, searching for shape, for purpose, but it didn't know what to do. Neither did he.

A gust of ash-laced wind rolled past, and he looked up.

Kaelir stood across the chaos, across the torn earth. Blood ran down the side of his face. One eye swollen shut. His sword was broken—only half a blade remained in his grip, but his eyes locked on Thane. Pleading and desperate. His eyes saying, *Help her. Please.*

Thane looked at him, but didn't move.

Lirien's fingers tightened on his arm. "Thane. Look at me."

He turned to her, away from Kaelir, away from Erynn.

Lirien's eyes were wide, glassed over and panicked, but somehow still steady and confident.

"You have to let go," she said, her voice level. "You *have to*. She gave you this chance. Don't waste it. There are too many of them…"

He turned back to Erynn. Her hand brushed his wrist, weakly—almost an apology.

Then he let go.

The threads of magic fell away from his grip. The glow on his skin receded. The moss blackened, curling in on itself. The pulse of wild power collapsed inward like a dying star.

He stood.

And then he ran.

Together, he and Lirien broke from the hillside. The roar of drakes overhead. The crash of Riders behind. The world narrowed to movement and breath and firelight flashing through smoke.

Smoke thickened. Shadows flickered. The ground rose beneath their feet—toward a broken ridge where a fallen Veilborn lay slumped against his mount. The drake twitched restlessly, still tethered, its flanks heaving from battle. Lirien didn't hesitate. She vaulted up, slashed the reins free with a single motion, and extended a hand.

Thane grabbed it.

Behind them, the screams grew sharper.

But then with the swift kick, Lirien pulled on the reins and the drake responded. The world fell away beneath them, and Thane clung to the saddle as the drake surged upward through the smoke. Lirien leaned forward, guiding with one hand, the other wrapped tight around a blood-stained rein. The beast's wings beat slow and heavy, each stroke scattering ash and embers in spirals behind them.

Beneath, the hillside blurred—movement and violence, fire and shadow.

Thane twisted, looking back.

The battle raged. The Veilborn held the line, but just barely. Bostick stood at the edge of a crumbling ridge, a drake at his back and a broken spear in hand. His armor was scorched, his face bloodied, but he was laughing. Laughing like he had nothing left to give but fury.

Kaelir still fought near Erynn's body. His sword gone, only using his fists now—tearing a Rider from its mount with brute strength, slamming it into the dirt. Another came. He didn't hesitate, but his movements slowed and one leg dragged.

And there—still crumpled near the scorched path where the Riders first broke through—lay Erynn.

Unmoving.

Her cloak twisted beneath her like a fallen banner, stained deep red at the center.

Thane didn't look away. Not this time. The wind tore at his hair, his skin, his lungs. But he kept watching, even as Lirien urged the drake higher.

"We'll make it worth it," she said.

It was either a promise or a prayer. But Thane didn't answer. His jaw clenched, and his fingers curled tighter around the saddle.

"We have to," he whispered.

The drake cut a wide arc through the smoke, wings straining against the weight of wind and ash.

Thane didn't speak. Neither did Lirien.

The air thinned the higher they climbed, until the noise below was just a murmur—the clash of steel, the crackle of flame, the screaming of things that had no names. From this height, the battle looked small, distant, and unreal, like a story told by someone who'd never lived it.

Smoke bled from the hills in thick, uneven pillars. Whole patches of the world were gone—reduced to scorched black veins carved into the land. The higher they rose, the more the Riders and Veilborn disappeared into the night.

Thane watched it all until the only thing left was the distant burst of flame from the drakes.

Then—nothing.

Just gray. The night stars above. And the heavy, endless beating of wings.

Lirien gave a sharp nudge with her heel, and the drake turned north. Toward Devendor.

Neither of them said it, but both knew what they were leaving behind.

The only thing that remained was the darkness ahead.

16

WHAT WAS LOST

THE DRAKE'S wings beat with slow, thunderous power, each motion rippling through Thane's spine like the deep toll of some forgotten bell. The creature's muscles rolled beneath its scaled hide, tight and warm with a pulse that wasn't quite natural, but wasn't quite animal either. There was something older burned there—ancient and as old as the peaks they crossed.

Thane held to the worn leather straps on the saddle, his fingers stiff from wind and cold. The air clawed at his coat, dragging his breath from his lungs. Arbelon stretched out far below them, shattered, scorched, and impossibly small. Villages were flattened to dust, rivers gone dry, and the roads broken like snapped threads on a dying loom.

He didn't speak, but neither did Lirien. The silence between them was its own language. A mixture of grief and determination wrapped up like an unspoken promise. They had no time for anything else now.

The drake angled east, climbing along the knife-edge of a mountain ridge where the wind howled like something wounded. Every dip and shift of the beast's spine reminded

Thane that this wasn't a trained mount, and it wasn't bred for riders, it just *tolerated* them. It had chosen not to throw him off… yet. Even now, he could feel its power vibrating beneath his bones, like riding the back of a storm not quite ready to break.

The wind shrieked around them, smoke veiled the horizon, and yet, for the first time in days, there was no one chasing them. Only what waited ahead.

Thane's knuckles whitened on the reins. Every mile they traveled away from the others weighed heavier than the last. He felt them all—Kaelir, Erynn, Bostick, and the other Veilborn they'd left behind. He saw them in every ember they passed, but he still didn't look back. He couldn't. Too much had been lost already.

His voice, when it came, was hoarse from cold and disuse.

"How do you know where to go?"

Lirien didn't answer right away. She shifted in her saddle, hair whipping behind her, eyes fixed on the shrouded horizon.

"I've been to the outer cliffs," she said at last. "A couple of years ago."

Thane looked at her. "Alone?"

"With a scouting party," she said. "We were planning a siege on Devendor, back when we still believed that was possible. The Elders thought there might be a weakness to be exploited."

She paused briefly, her eye looking off in the distance.

"There wasn't."

She leaned forward slightly, as if the wind might carry her memories forward ahead of them.

"But then there were whispers of something older. Something hidden beneath it."

Thane nodded in silence, letting her words settle between them like ash.

The drake banked, and the rising sun glinted off its scales—black stone laced with veins of dim violet light, like obsidian filled with lightning too old to strike again.

Behind them, their past trailed away.

Ahead, in the distant north, the peaks around Devendor waited like teeth in the sky.

They flew on.

The air grew thinner as the day wore on, slicing colder the higher they climbed. Beneath them, the world fell away into scarred terrain—shadows of forests long devoured by fire, hills reduced to glitched grids of ash and rootless soil. Here and there, Thane glimpsed what might've once been towns. Now just blackened outlines, like the ghosts of cities that had been forgotten even by the wind.

They didn't speak. There was nothing left to say.

The drake's flight slowed near midday. Its breath came heavier. Lirien murmured a word into its ear, and it banked lower, gliding down through a veil of mist, landing on a cleft in the rock where a narrow stream spilled over moss-covered stones. They dismounted, sore and spent.

The clearing was small, surrounded by warped pines that bent in strange directions, as if pulled toward something unseen. The stream gurgled cold and clean through the hollow, cutting a thin scar of light across the grey stone.

Thane knelt at the water's edge. He cupped his hands and drank, and as the ripples settled, he caught his reflection in the stream, except it wasn't just him. Not entirely. For a flicker of a moment, the face that stared back wore his eyes but not his mind—something darker moving beneath the surface, pupils too wide, mouth almost smiling.

It was Echo.

He blinked, and the image snapped back. Now only

reflecting his face. Hollow-eyed and bone-tired. Too many miles behind, too many ahead.

A breath brushed the back of his neck, and Thane twisted around. But there was nothing there. Only Lirien, crouched a few feet away, running a wet cloth over the drake's flank, her expression unreadable.

She must've seen something in his face as her eyes turned to him, flashing concern. But she didn't ask or press him, instead, she just walked over and placed a hand on his shoulder. Light, steady, and real.

Then, without a word, she turned away and mounted the drake again. Thane followed.

The drake spread its wings, and with a single push, they rose once more into the sky, traveling for the better part of the day. The sun had dipped low by the time they reached the hollow. It was little more than a pocket carved into the shoulder of the mountain—flat enough to land, quiet enough to feel untouched. Gnarled pines ringed the space like sentinels, their branches twisted by altitude and wind. Fog drifted low across the stone, swirling at their ankles in pale threads.

The drake settled with a huff and folded its wings. Its flanks shimmered with faint light—exhausted but alive. They dismounted again in silence, and, for a while, there was only the sound of their movements. Lirien gathered kindling from the wind-dried brush, while Thane unbuckled the satchel of dried provisions slung behind the saddle.

No words passed between them.

Not yet.

He watched her work. The practiced motion of her hands. The sharp way she moved, but always with purpose. She knelt, striking flint to steel, and the spark caught quickly, the fire dancing in the center of a makeshift ring of stones.

Thane crouched beside her. Close, but not too close. His voice came quietly.

"Why are you so good to me?"

She didn't look up, but no words came either.

He hesitated, fumbling for the next words.

"Hey, I…"

Thane trailed off, rubbing the back of his neck, staring at the fire. The words didn't come. At least not the right words, not like he'd hoped they would.

"It doesn't matter," he muttered.

But it *did*, and he knew it.

"What?" she asked, warmly—more so than he deserved from her.

He continued to watch her stoke the fire, lay in new kindling. Nurturing the fire as she was him.

With a calming breath, he continued.

"What happened in Asmenson…" He paused, looking at how her hair fell on her shoulders. "I can't stop seeing it… you. The way you looked at me after."

He reached over, gently turning her, and met their eyes for the first time since landing. "I don't think I ever said it. I'm sorry. I should've, I just… I didn't know how."

Lirien reached out, placing a finger to his lips.

"Stop."

She said it gently, but firmly, cutting him off with the same ease as she would draw a blade.

"You didn't destroy me. Not really. Asmenson was already dying. Same as the Heart. What happened… it wasn't your choice. It was this world's sickness, festering through us all."

She lowered her hand, firelight casting her features in amber and shadow.

"And your magic? I never held that against you. Not then. Not now. We all do what we must. And you," her voice softened, "you've proven who you are. At least to me."

Their eyes held one another in a quiet embrace. Knowing. Acknowledgment.

The silence hung thick between them, until he swallowed hard. His next words came hoarse and uncertain.

"There are things I should remember. But I can't."

She tilted her head slightly, listening, her eyes never leaving him now.

"My mother's face. Her voice. It's like… it's gone. Like something's scraping pieces of her out of me, and I can't stop it. Maybe it was the Fae."

He paused.

"Or maybe it's my disease, finally finding me here, too."

He looked down at his hands, chapped and shaking slightly in the cold.

"But I don't want that to happen to you. I don't want you to forget. I want you to remember things. Things that matter."

And then, quietly, he reached into his pocket taking out a small, gold ring—worn and simple. He held it a moment, just long enough for the firelight to catch on its surface, then he placed it in her palm.

It was her mother's ring. The one she had buried outside Trosten, trying to bury her grief with it. The one Thane had secreted away, kept, and carried across every mile since.

Lirien stared at it. Frozen.

"I went back," she whispered. "I tried to find it. But it was gone… I thought it was lost." Her voice cracked. "But you… you kept this safe for me? All this time?"

He shrugged—his cheeks reddening.

"I don't know why. I just knew it mattered."

In that instant, everything between them changed.

Lirien leaned forward, fingers still curled around the ring—and kissed him.

It wasn't delicate. It wasn't planned. It was full of exhaustion and longing and heat and silence. It was the kind of kiss people only give when they've already made up their minds.

When it broke, she stayed close. Forehead against his. Breath steady.

She didn't smile. She didn't pull away.

And neither did he.

He took the ring and slid it gently onto her finger.

She was *his*, and he—somehow—was hers.

"We'll come back to this," she said.

He nodded. "No matter what."

Her eyes held his, steady and unflinching. "No matter what."

The words weren't loud, but they carried like an oath.

They didn't linger. The hollow would fade to shadow soon, and the road ahead was waiting, but for the first time, Thane carried something with him besides the fight.

They flew hard for the rest of the day. Not lingering on the words from the hollow—only the wind, the beating of wings, and the steady rhythm of Thane's hand on the drake's neck. Whenever the creature began to falter, Thane reached for his Wild Magic. Each time, the magic resisted him at first—sluggish and reluctant—before spilling into the drake in flickers of strength he couldn't afford to waste. Every pulse of it stole something from him. His arms trembled, his vision narrowed, and, still, he pushed it on, refusing to let it land.

By nightfall, the mountains fell away into a knife-edged

cliff that ringed the world. Below, black space opened into an ocean of mist. The air here tasted thin and metallic, charged like a storm before lightning.

Lirien guided the drake lower, wings brushing the cliff-side, their approach lit only by the creature's pale wing-light and the silver wash of the moon.

And then Devendor appeared.

The fortress rose directly from the plateau's spine, a sheer wall of blackstone that grew upward from the bones of the mountain. Its silhouette cut the moon in two. Water-falls poured down its craggy face in thin silver ribbons, vanishing into the fog far below. Each spill of water caught the moonlight as if threaded with quicksilver—and yet, the sound of them never reached the riders.

The natural cliffs morphed into great barrier walls that climbed in staggered tiers up the mountainside, ring upon ring, each studded with towers that gleamed with a reddish light, like torches where no fire should be. The glow moved wrong, almost liquid, as if alive. From the walls came the faintest hum—low and steady, a pulse like a heartbeat felt in the bones rather than heard in the ear. Incredible stone bridges reached across the chasm, connecting the great city of Devendor to the landscape beyond.

At the lowest tier, the front gate yawned open: a towering arch of blackstone and iron, wide enough for ten Riders abreast. Its surface was etched with runes that glim-mered like old embers, the shapes shifting when looked at too long. Black-armored Riders moved in and out through the gate in unbroken rhythm, their formation as precise as clockwork. Their armor drank the moonlight, gleaming only where red sigils burned faintly along their gauntlets.

From here, the city seemed alive, its veins pulsing with movement, its wards humming with unseen power, and it radiated from the fortress like heat from a forge. The air pressed against Thane's skin, all but confirming Echo's presence somewhere beyond. A fact confirmed by the watch on his wrist that throbbed steadily now. Not just warning—*calling*.

Lirien banked the drake wide, skirting the fortress's shadow until they reached a crumbling ridge at the far northern edge at the base of the plateau. It was awash in darkness, nothing remarkable to note.

She dismounted, boots crunching on frost, and scanned the wall of rock before them.

"The books deep in the archives referenced this spot. They called it the High King's Escape," she whispered. "From the first days of the kingdom. Abandoned and sealed millennia ago."

She pressed her palm flat to the stone.

"If the writings were right…" Her breath clouded in the cold air. "It may still remain."

Lirien kept her palm pressed to the stone, eyes half-closed, listening to something beneath the surface, but the rock stayed cold and unyielding.

"It's here," she murmured, stepping back. "I can sense it. But it's locked. Old wards—dead ones. I can—"

"Let me," Thane said, stepping forward before she could finish. His hand went to the wall, fingers spread against the stone's chill.

The reaction was immediate. Crimson light flared along the rock's surface, jagged and violent, bleeding through ancient carvings like molten glass through cracks. Heat seared his skin, sharp enough to blister. He yanked his hand back with a hiss, cradling it to his chest.

Lirien started toward him. "Thane—"

"No," he growled. "I've got this."

He pressed his palm to the wall again, probing it slower this time. He reached for the magic, drawing it out of himself until his chest felt hollow, until his bones ached with the pull.

For a moment, it *worked*. The stone rippled under his hand. A red shimmer coalesced into the faint outline of a doorway, runes unfurling like black ivy along its frame. The hum in the air deepened, pressing against his skull.

Then something pushed back. Hard.

The magic surged the wrong way, flooding back into him like a snapped tide. It slammed through his mind and spine, hammering him in the skull with the force of a cinder block. He flew backward, hit the ground, and the air punched out of him in a ragged gasp. Then the world tilted. His limbs twitched in sharp, involuntary spasms, the taste of copper on his lips as blood trickled hot from his ear, down his jaw.

Lirien's voice cut through the ringing, but faint, like she was speaking from the bottom of a lake.

"Thane! Thane—stay with me!"

He tried to answer, but his throat locked. His vision tunneled, collapsing inward until only the red shimmer of the doorway remained. The magic's heat still burned in his palm, even as it slipped away from him.

He wasn't being thrown back because he'd failed. He was being *taken*.

His watch flickered once. The doorway's glow pulsed red, brighter and brighter, then collapsed into a red ring and winked out.

And then the world tore sideways. The cold stone was gone. The smell of frost and firelight, gone. Lirien's face, gone.

Only the rush of empty air, the crushing weight in his chest, and a final, desperate thought—

Not now. Not when we were so close.

Everything went black.

17

———

FRACTURED REALITY

Thane woke in a blur.

There were no voices and no movement. Only the ache in his bones and a dull, alien throb behind his eyes, pulsing in time with his heartbeat.

Something wet traced the curve of his jaw. He lifted a hand to it, his fingers brushing his skin that had gone cold, and they came away dark and sticky—blood. It looked almost black in the thin, sickly ashen light leaking through the blinds.

The smell followed—burnt plastic, sharp and chemical, tangled with something sweet and cloying. Smoke. For a heartbeat, he thought he heard singing, faint and far away, the kind of sound you couldn't be sure you'd heard at all. Then it was gone, swallowed by the low, insect hum of the lights, and the faint tick of the wall clock.

He was back in his room. He was back on Earth.

The VR headset clung crooked to his face, one strap twisted, hanging by a single ear. Its dead weight tugged at him, the screen black as stone, as if it had never been alive at all.

175

A sound at the door, soft at first, then the shift of weight on old floorboards. The door opened just far enough for light from the hallway to spill across the carpet, and his mother stepped in, stopping mid-step. Her gaze dropping to the dark headset, then to the blood. Her breath caught sharp in her throat, eyes fixed on the smear of red across his cheek and the thin trails drying along his neck. Panic seemed to hollow her face from the inside.

"Thane…" Her voice wavered. "What are you doing?"

The words hung in the air, too loud for the small room. Her gaze snapped to the headset. Before he could stop her, she crossed the room and pulled it from his hands. She turned it over, fingers tracing the casing, then stopped. A faint, jagged crack split the lens from corner to corner.

"Thane…" Her voice was softer now, almost careful. "This thing is broken. It hasn't worked since before you went to the hospital. Before the last time you used it."

He shook his head. "No. I fixed it."

She crouched beside the gaming rig, her hand spinning it toward the light. There was no power cord. Where one should've been, the port gaped empty, the edges furred with dust.

"It's not even plugged in," she said. "I've got the cord in my dresser. I took it out weeks ago."

The words seemed to hollow the air around him. The faint hum of the lights pressed against his ears, louder now —almost a vibration. The smell of smoke from moments ago still clung to the back of his throat. The room felt tilted, like the floor wasn't quite where it had been.

Her voice stayed calm, too calm. "Honey… I think you're seeing things. This isn't real."

It landed like a slap. Something tore loose in his chest.

He could hear his own heartbeat now, fast and heavy. He *knew* it was real. It had to be, and that meant there was only one explanation. She started to speak, but he cut her off, his words low, certain. "Don't you see? It was never the headset." His gaze locked on hers. "It's me. I've been doing it the whole time."

Her hand reached for his—not just comfort, but as if she could pull him back into the real world. He didn't pull away. He needed her close, he needed to bring her with him. The room seemed to contract, the walls drawing in.

"It's real, mom," he whispered. "The magic is real. Arbelon isn't a game."

For a long moment, neither of them moved. The air between them felt stretched, thin enough to tear.

Jane's fingers tightened slightly around his hand. Her voice, when it came, was quiet, almost swallowed by the hum of the lights.

"You sound like your father."

Thane stilled, his pulse still hammering from before. "What do you mean?"

Her gaze drifted past him, like she was looking through the wall and into some old, far-off memory. "In his last weeks... he would talk about places that didn't exist." She swallowed. "Names I'd never heard before, but I never forgot them."

Her eyes shifted back to his, hesitant, like speaking the words aloud might make them dangerous.

"Salile. Devendor. Felderwin."

The names hit him like cold water.

He leaned forward, almost too close. "I've been there. I've walked their streets." The words tumbled out faster, ragged. "They're real, Mom. All of it. Arbelon is real—the people are real. Lirien is real. And they need me. I'm more alive there than here. If I can get back, I can save them. All of them. Even Dad." His breath hitched. "I can save him too. You don't understand—he's not gone. He's *there*."

Jane's mouth opened, then closed. Her expression shifted in small, conflicting beats—denial, fear, something else he couldn't name.

"That's not possible," she said at last. But even as she said it, her voice faltered.

He searched her face, looking for the crack in her certainty. Her eyes shifted—something in them softening, just for a moment. He couldn't tell if it was belief, pity, or something else entirely, but whatever it was, it felt perilously close to hope. If there was ever a chance to convince her, to get her to believe, it was now or never. So he dove in, no holds barred.

"I think I can take you there," he whispered. "Then you'll see. You'll believe me."

She didn't look away. Her eyes glassed over, a single tear slipping down her cheek. Words formed on her lips, but nothing came.

"Just see it," he said, the words coming softer now, almost a plea. "Just once. Then you'll know. Then you'll finally believe me."

Her thumb brushed over his knuckles, slow and absent, like she was afraid to break the moment.

He swallowed hard, his hand holding hers a bit tighter.

"There's someone I need you to meet," he said, his voice catching. "Her name is Lirien. I..." He almost laughed at the absurdity, but the truth pressed out of him anyway. "I think I love her."

Jane's lips parted, but no sound came, even now. She just looked at him, long enough for him to feel the weight of it, like she was trying to memorize his face.

Then she reached up and brushed the hair from his forehead. "I haven't seen this part of you in so long." Her voice cracked on the last word.

"I love you more than life itself," she said at last. Her

hands lingered against his cheeks, holding him still, her thumbs stroking once before falling away. "If you can still love someone—if you think you can help these people—then go."

"But what about you?" His voice was almost boyish, raw. "Are you coming?"

She hesitated, just long enough for him to notice. Her gaze shifted, and when she looked back at him, her smile was small and sad. "Of course I'm coming," she said, voice warm but fragile. Her fingertips trailed along his temple like she was committing it to memory. "I'd follow you anywhere."

He didn't know if she meant it. Didn't know if she was humoring him, or if something in her had finally shifted. But the way she said it, the way she held him—he let himself believe.

He closed his eyes, breathed deep. The watch on his wrist seemed to pulse with his heartbeat, each throb stronger than the last. He reached for it, not with his hands, but with the part of him that Arbelon had changed. That Arbelon had *made*.

He called the Wild Magic.

He didn't open his eyes right away. He just breathed, slow and deep, and let the warmth gather in his chest until it felt too big to contain. The pulse from the watch spread through his veins, searing and sweet, and the air in the room began to hum.

Golden light bled out from beneath his skin. At first, it was just in his hands, the glow pushing between his fingers, but then it spilled wider, pouring into the air like sunrise caught in water. The walls wavered. Shadows bent away from him. The warmth swelled into something almost physical, pressing close, wrapping him and his mother in a cocoon of light. He could feel her fingers tighten around his. The glow shifted and shimmered, not harsh, not blinding—alive. It breathed with him. Somewhere deep inside it, there was a note of silver. A flicker. Static in the warmth. The edges of the room folded in on themselves, their corners unthreading like loose cloth.

He opened his eyes and the world broke.

Light distorted. The floor fell away without moving. Shapes collapsed and reformed in the same heartbeat. When the glow thinned, they were standing on black stone dusted with frost, cliffs rising like sheer blades all around them. Above, the jagged crown of a fortress bit into the night sky.

Jane blinked, her eyes wide. She turned slowly, taking in the air—sharp and cold enough to taste.

"This is…" She hesitated, her voice barely a whisper. "Devendor."

Lirien froze, her eyes wide. She was staring at Jane since she'd just appeared from thin air, and her voice came thin. "How do you know this place?"

Jane's gaze stayed on the fortress, stepping away from Thane. "We used to come here… Well, not physically. But your father would tell me all about these places—these wonderful places. Devendor. Towers the reached to the sky. And lakes of light." She wiped at her cheek. "I thought it was just something his mind created… a way to cope. He even said I'd be here someday. I thought it was just him losing his mind."

"Mom, he wasn't. It's all real," Thane said.

Jane's gaze drifted from the sheer cliffs to the young woman at Thane's side.

"This is Lirien," Thane said, his voice low but steady. "The one I told you about."

Lirien's eyes widened, but there was no suspicion in

them—only surprise and a quick, bright smile. "This is your mother."

Before Thane could answer, Jane stepped forward and wrapped her arms around Lirien. The embrace was instinctive, fierce, the kind that comes from gratitude too big for words.

Lirien returned it without hesitation, holding Jane as if they'd known each other far longer than the space of a breath. "It's an honor to meet you," she said into Jane's shoulder. "He's… he can be a handful, but you probably know that."

Jane's laugh broke in the middle, turning into something wetter. She pulled back just enough to look at Lirien's face, brushing a strand of hair from her cheek like she was memorizing it. "You're even more beautiful than he said."

Lirien flushed, smiling through the faint shimmer in her eyes. "I'm glad you're here."

Jane's voice caught. "So am I." She looked between them, her hand finding Thane's for just a second. "More than you know."

For Thane, it was like watching two halves of his life meet—his world on Earth and his world in Arbelon—and instead of clashing, they folded into each other as if they'd always belonged.

Jane nodded once, almost to herself, then turned her attention back to the cliff wall.

"Do you know what this place is?" she asked them.

Lirien nodded. "The High King's Escape."

"And you know how to enter?" Jane asked.

"We're having a little trouble with that," Thane answered.

"I think I can help with that. Your father spoke of this place many times," Jane said, and then turned and walked to the cliff wall. She searched the stone, running her fingers across it. "Here it is," she whispered. Her fingers reached into a crack, twisting.

A sound, soft but deep, rolled out from within. Runes shimmered under her palm, tracing a slow silver arc that spiraled outward. Light cascaded across the wall, pulling itself into the shape of an arched doorway.

The stone shuddered, cracked, and slid away to reveal a dark passage beyond.

Jane stepped forward without looking back.

Thane glanced at Lirien, who still hadn't taken her eyes off Jane.

He followed—Lirien at his side.

And for the first time, he didn't have to walk into the dark alone.

18

CORRUPTED CODE

THE DOOR YAWNED OPEN, and Jane was already inside, her hand reaching for something just beyond the threshold.

Thane slowed at the entrance, his fingers brushing the glimmering glyphs cut deep into the lintel. The marks were older than Devendor itself, metallic seams pressed into the rock like veins of a different world. They gave off no light, yet seemed to breathe under his touch, a faint pulse traveling into his fingertips and cascading up the archway. He drew his hand back sharply, as if the stone still recognized him, but had decided to let him pass.

Lirien stepped in beside him, her eyes following the runes that marked the entrance.

There was a faint hum—low, steady, and wrong. The sound faded when they moved forward, as though the place had closed its eyes again.

Inside, Jane wrenched a torch from its cradle. The sconce was a relic, iron blackened over the centuries, the metal etched with the same strange inlay as the lintel. She struck the flint hanging from the scone once, twice, and then the torch caught with a thin gasp of light. The flame didn't rise so much as lean forward, drawn into the darkness ahead. For a moment, it warped the glyph-light on the lintel, twisting the patterns into shapes he couldn't quite name.

Jane adjusted her grip on the torch without looking at them. "South tunnel curves right, then drops," she murmured—too precise, too certain.

Lirien's eyes cut to her, quick and sharp, but she said nothing.

The tunnel beyond was raw stone, hacked and torn by tools that had cared nothing for symmetry. Deep grooves raked along the walls, the edges sharp as if cut yesterday. The air clung cold in his throat, with an under-taste of metal and rain.

Thane glanced at his mother. "He said you'd be here someday."

She turned just enough for the torchlight to find her face, the glow picking out the fine lines around her eyes.

"And here I am." She tilted her head slightly. "What now?"

The question hung between them. There were a dozen things he could have asked—should have asked—but the words stayed buried instead. He gave the smallest nod to the tunnel ahead, and they pressed on.

They moved as one into the dark. The torchlight pushed a narrow wedge into it, but the shadows clung stubbornly to the walls, as if they had weight. The first fork came within a dozen paces. The tunnel split into two identical mouths, the same rough stone, the same lean of the ceiling, the same dust along the floor. Jane didn't even slow. She took the left path, her voice low, almost distracted.

"Down is not always forward."

Thane's jaw tightened. His father had said that many times—long before this moment had ever occurred. And somehow she not only remembered it, but knew its meaning to this precise time.

The tunnels kept shifting. Some sloped down, some rose, some bent so subtly he only realized it when the air changed temperature. At times, they looped in on themselves, bringing them past the same knot of rock more than once, but Jane always picked a turn, and finally the repetition broke.

Lirien stayed close to the wall, eyes flicking between a parchment Erynn had given her from the archives and the route Jane took. After the third or fourth fork, she stopped pretending she was leading and stowed the parchment, choosing to follow.

The walls bore no marks, and Jane pushed on without any map. Only the memories and mumblings of a madman leading the way. They rounded another corner and the wall to Thane's right flickered—a sheet of black glass jutted from the wall like a buried mirror. The torchlight barely touched it, but it was enough for him to see a reflection in its surface, a face warped with eyes hollowed, and a mouth curved in a smile he'd never made.

Echo stared back at him.

He blinked, but then it was gone as quickly as it had surfaced. Now just a drab surface of rock hewn long ago.

Jane didn't look back. She kept walking, pulling them forward.

In the next few paces, the rough stone began to change. The cuts in the wall smoothed out, and the torchlight no longer caught on jagged edges. The floor flattened until each step felt unnaturally level, like walking a line drawn by a machine. The angles of the walls were now sharp enough to feel deliberate. This wasn't built by miners.

Lirien slowed. Eyes moving from side to side.

"This is too easy…" she murmured, her voice low and restrained.

Then the tunnels ended without warning. One turn later and the corridor opened like into the gaping mouth of a cavern, swallowing the torchlight and replacing it with its own glow—cold, fractured, and wrong.

They stepped into a chamber so vast that the walls seemed to vanish before the ceiling did. The floor was polished obsidian, black as still water, veined with hairline cracks of pale crystal that pulsed faintly, like a heartbeat too far away to hear.

At the chamber's center stood jagged monoliths of blackened stone and crystal that rose in a perfect ring, each one scarred with deep runes that bled dull light. The tallest stone loomed in the middle, its surface carved with grooves so deep they looked like they'd been clawed there by some-thing massive. The light from within it shifted, almost alive, as if trying to push through the rock and reach them.

He'd seen something like this before—at Skyreach Henge—but this… this was different. Darker. Not touched by open air or wind. This one had been buried, hidden, smothered beneath the weight of an ancient city, and still it pulsed.

Jane's voice was hushed. "Where are we?"

Lirien didn't take her eyes off the ring of stones. "A place of ancient power."

The words had barely left her mouth when the watch on Thane's wrist flared to life—violently, searing white, its pulse beating in perfect rhythm with the crystal veins threading through the floor.

Thane moved without thinking, drifting to the wall, wanting to create some distance between him and what-ever called to him. The obsidian walls shimmered when his palm touched it, rippling outward in concentric waves.

Lirien's voice was sharp now.

"Thane… what is this place?"

His eyes tracked the nearest stone, the runes crawling faintly like molten metal cooling in water.

"It has to be another portal. Like on Skyreach."

Jane stepped closer to the tallest monolith, unafraid, the torchlight sliding over her face.

The chamber shuddered. Cracks of light spidered through the walls—pale and jagged, like lightning trapped behind glass. The edges of the stones began to smear, glitching sideways before snapping back. The hum in the floor deepened, resonating in his ribs until his own heartbeat struggled to keep its rhythm.

The pulse from the Henge built in the floor, low at first, then swelling until it filled the air like a second heartbeat. The runes on the tallest stone flared, flooding the chamber with a cold, argent glow. Shadows bent away from it. The walls shuddered, fractured light bleeding through seams in the stone.

Jane stumbled. The torch nearly fell from her grasp, but she steadied herself. Her breath came in ragged gasps as her body lurched forward, flickering, breaking apart in stutters of movement. One moment she was whole, the next her outline bled into the air like wet ink smeared by an unseen hand. The air around her went suddenly cold, raising the hairs on Thane's arms.

"It's… too much," she breathed. "I can't… what's happening…"

Thane was already moving. He caught her before she fell, lowering them both to the cold floor. The torch rolled away, its light spilling in a thin arc that danced against the polished walls.

Her head rested against his chest, breath shallow, each inhale catching like it hurt. Tears of blood traced thin lines down her cheeks, dark against the trembling light. It streamed from her eyes, her nose, the corner of her mouth —each drop vanishing before it touched the floor. Her face rippled, a thousand hairline fractures running through her features like cracked glass.

"No, no, no——" He pressed his palm to her chest, just over her heart. He reached for the Wild Magic, for that deep, unsteady current that had healed the others below Felderwin. It surged up fast—too fast—white fire raced down his arm into her.

Come on… work.

For a heartbeat her flickering steadied, her breath caught, and something like color began to return to her face.

It's working…

Then the Henge's pulse slammed back through him like a wall, snapping the magic out of his grip. The glow in his hand guttered to nothing.

Her gaze found his, steady for a moment despite the shaking. "You were always…" Her voice faltered, and she blinked hard, trying to keep her gaze fixed on him. "His light. And mine. Always."

Her hand came up, fingertips brushing his cheek in a gesture so familiar it tore something open inside him.

"And now look at you," she said, not with disappointment, but wonder. Pride. Love.

He swallowed hard, words jagged in his throat. "I'm sorry. I shouldn't have brought you here. This is my fault."

Her smile was small but certain. "No… this is where I wanted to be. With you."

Her breath slowed. Her eyelids fluttered once, twice. Then she was still.

He stayed there, bent over her, holding her as if through sheer will he could hold the breath in her. The hum of the Henge and the shattering light faded into nothing. All that existed was the weight of her in his arms and the cold certainty that she was slipping away.

Lirien had knelt nearby, her hand half-extended toward Jane, but she stopped, her face pale and unreadable.

A shimmer along the edge of Jane's form began. The faintest pull upward, like unseen threads drawing her away.

Not decay or fading. This was something else.

The edges of her form started to unravel, curling upward into the still air as gray, weightless motes. They shimmered once, twice, then drifted away like ash in a wind that didn't exist. Piece by piece, she vanished, until his arms closed on nothing but the echo of her shape.

His sat there for a moment, his arms outstretched. The emptiness struck like a blow—his breath left him in a sharp, soundless gasp. He stayed frozen there, unable to move, leaving only the hollow ache in his chest and the cold stone under his knees. The chamber was too quiet. The hum of the Henge had thinned to a brittle, static edge.

Something shuddered in the air behind him, like glass flexing under invisible hands. He turned his head, slow at first. The space wavered, and light bent inward. From the distortion, a shadow stepped free—no footfall, no breath—coalescing from air and static, as though the world was rendering something it was never meant to hold. It wore a shape, but only enough to mock one. Limbs fractured and reformed as it moved, and the face was wrong—too fluid, too knowing.

"Thane," it said. The voice was layered, echoing against itself, pulled through a broken channel. "I brought you to this henge… just like he did to me."

It paused, head tilting as though studying him. The edges of its form flickered.

"And now look at you."

The same words Jane had just spoken. But here they were split, bent, and wrong—played back in his mind with a lag, folding over themselves in static.

And now look at you.

And now look at you.

And now look at you.

Lirien's scream tore through the chamber, bringing Thane back.

The tallest stone flared, pure and searing white, and the rest followed, the henge igniting in a cascading burst. The pulse slammed through the floor, and Thane's watch erupted in a burst of sparks, the crystal face shattering and falling to the ground in a cascade of shards.

And then the world broke.

The light from the henge hadn't fully faded when the air folded again. The distortion that had shaped Echo only moments ago thickened and deepened until his form was there, full and undeniable. He was no longer wearing a face of shadow, but a face of something familiar and defined.

Lirien staggered back, her hand still half-raised from when Jane had vanished. She didn't get more than a step before Echo's hand lifted, lazily and almost bored, and shadows erupted from the floor. They wrapped around her midsection and throat, binding her in midair. She choked out a gasp, boots kicking at nothing, voice held silent.

"Now you know," Echo said, his voice rippling through the chamber. "Now you know what it feels like to lose all that you love. Just like what you did to Lirien in Asmenson. Just like you did to Kaelir… Now *you* feel it."

Thane spun toward him, magic already surging. The heat in his veins threatened to spill free, but Echo only tightened his hold on Lirien, the shadows constricting until her breath hitched.

"I didn't stop you," Echo went on. "I let you come. I had her bring you to this place—just like I knew she would. Because only *your* magic can open the way. Only you can help me seal the fate of these worlds."

His gaze was sharp, unblinking. "You're not like them—the Arbeloneans." The word *Arbeloneans* came out like rot on his tongue. "You're like me. I'm a part of you. I'm a part of your father. We are both from one, and like me, you don't just want to survive. You want to *save* someone."

The pulse of the henge seemed to deepen, as if listening.

Echo's smile cut thin. "Open the gate, Thane. Open it, and I will give her back to you—your mother, my wife. There is still time—this doesn't have to be the end."

The words sank their hooks deep, deeper than he'd ever imagined words could. For a long moment, Thane couldn't look at Echo. He stared at Lirien, her teeth bared in defiance even as she fought for breath. He looked to the ancient stones throbbing with power, seeking what he had. And all of this, at the place where his mother had vanished, literally into thin air. It was too much, too convenient.

"This is a trick," he said, low.

"Of course it is," Echo replied, leaning in slightly. "But does that matter? If it works?"

The henge stirred around Thane, the stone thrumming, the air bending. Finally, he relented. Wild Magic leapt to his call, spilling uncontrolled into the space. The space around him glitched, colors bending at the edges of sight.

"Thane—don't!" Lirien's cry cut sharp, but he didn't answer.

His feet were already moving. He stepped into the circle. The runes along the stones ignited, their light pulsing in time with his heartbeat. The floor shook, heavy from somewhere deep below and high above, and light peeled from the walls like old skin.

Reality tore down the center—forming a door. Beyond it was a glade shrouded in a golden mist. At its center, something pulsed, alive and immense.

The Womb of the Heart.

And Thane stepped toward it.

1 9

ASH AND BLOOM

THE PORTAL COLLAPSED BEHIND him with a sound like shattering glass swallowed by water, and he stood in the glade. When he'd last seen this place, it was bathed in living light, but it now stood before him hollowed out, bleeding, and barely holding on.

Crystal-veined trees still arched overhead like the ribs of a cathedral, but their trunks were bowed, some split down the middle, their veins dulled to a sullen gray. Silver leaves drifted through the air, fewer now, some dissolving into black ash before touching the ground. And the pale stone path lay cracked underfoot, glyphs flickering like dying embers. Shadows seeped into the fractures, spreading in slow, deliberate tendrils.

Above the shallow pool in the center, the Heart still hung in its cradle of woven light, but the weave was frayed, its strands sparking and snapping into nothing. The womb itself pulsed weakly, each beat a struggle, its once-bright surface split by wide, jagged cracks that wept sparks into the water below.

Suspended within, Thane's father remained—frail and half-conscious, his body slumped in the dim glow.

The air carried the faint tang of burnt metal and old magic, the steady hum replaced by a labored, uneven throb that seemed to echo inside Thane's own chest. Beneath him, the ground at his feet pixelated in patches, flickering between stone and void as if reality itself were being eaten away.

Thane whispered, "This place is dying…"

Thane's words hung in the air, swallowed by the labored throb of the failing Heart.

But then a shadow slid across the far edge of the glade —not cast by tree or vine, but moving on its own, stretching and curling against the broken lattice. It bled upward, pulling into the shape of a man, sleek and black-veined. The edges of the figure glitching like a frame caught between moments.

And the face—

Thane's breath locked in his throat. It was his father's face, but not. The eyes burned too dark, the mouth held in a perpetual half-smile that didn't belong to the man in the womb, the man he'd known and remembered. It was a perfect mirror, but cracked down the middle, every flaw sharpened.

"Welcome home," Echo said, voice smooth as glass dragged across stone.

He lifted one hand, casual and carefree, as the air beside him shimmered. From that shimmer, Lirien was wrenched into view, bound in coils of flickering tendrils that writhed like living script. Her feet barely touched the ground. She struggled once, breath catching, but made no sound. Her eyes found Thane's, wide and unblinking, the terror there speaking louder than any scream.

"You almost broke it once," Echo went on, stepping

forward. Each movement sent a ripple through the shadows clinging to him, distorting the glade around his form. "Now we can finish what you started years ago. I can finally realize my true potential—thanks to you."

He turned his gaze toward the Heart.

The tendrils binding Lirien tightened, lifting her higher as he extended his other hand toward the womb. The light inside shivered, then bent toward him in thin streams, drawn out like silk threads into his palm. As the power flowed, the fractures in his form began to knit, the glitches smoothing out, and his stance grew steadier, more solid.

The womb gave a deep, shuddering pulse, then dimmed, the once-luminous glow paling further. Sparks continued to shower down from its surface like dying fireflies, each one winking out before reaching the water. The hiss of siphoned light filled the glade, a sound somewhere between breath and static.

Thane took a step toward Echo, and at that moment the world seemed to answer. It started in his chest, a pulse so deep it rattled his ribs. Then another, sharper, threading down his arms and legs like molten wire. He staggered, clutching at the ache blooming behind his sternum.

The nanovirions were awake. He could feel them soldiering through his veins.

And they weren't just reacting, they were *reaching*. Outward, into the lattice, into the fractured womb, into the faint spark that was his father's life. He felt the connection snap into place like a circuit completing. It wasn't magic or science, it was *both*, interwoven.

A low hum rose from the ground, vibrating through his boots, through his bones. Up in the cradle, his father's head shifted ever so slightly. One eye cracked opened. It was cloudy, unfocused, but it found Thane, and held him.

There were no words. None needed. The moment

poured into him full and unrestrained—the truth, raw and absolute.

The magic had never been his alone. It was theirs. A network. A living design that spanned Arbelon's heart and blood and sky and through the veil. The nanovirions weren't a weapon, they were the bridge. His father had been the source, the anchor, and together they were the answer. But now, strand by strand, that legacy was bleeding into Echo's waiting hands.

"It was always you," Thane murmured, his eye on his father, his voice breaking. "You were the source… and the key."

Above, the siphoning deepened, the womb's glow collapsing inward. Echo's grin widened. The hum in the glade was building—threading through Thane, tying him to the lattice, to his father, to *everything*. It was fragile, a moment that could break one way or the other.

He took another step forward, a glance at Lirien… and hesitated.

It was all that Echo needed.

The world cracked open. A spear woven of shadow erupted from the air itself, slamming into Thane's abdomen. It punched through flesh and bone with a wet, jarring crunch, hot pain detonating up his spine.

"I will take what little is left of you too," Echo hissed, his voice curling like smoke through Thane's ear.

Thane folded around the wound, knees buckling. Warmth gushed over his fingers as he clutched at it— blood, yes, but laced with something hotter, something stranger. The edges of the injury flickered like torn code, pixels shearing away and snapping back as the nanovirions surged to contain the damage.

But they weren't fast enough.

"You are weak," Echo snarled, stepping closer, the

shadow spike still buried in Thane's gut. "You were never meant to survive. You were the tether to this place. *I* was the true creation."

Lirien's scream cut through the glade, sharp but muffled and distorted, like it came from another world. She writhed in her bindings, fighting to resist, but the flickering tendrils around her pulled tighter, biting into her skin as blood oozed out. Her eyes locked with Thane's, wide with terror, but her voice was swallowed in the static like it never existed.

In the next instant, the shadow spike dissolved into smoke, retreating into Echo's hand, but the wound it left behind throbbed like it was still being pierced, and Thane's breath came in ragged pulls. His vision swam. But beyond the pain—through the haze—he saw him again in the Womb.

His father, suspended in the lattice, light leaking from his body like water through a broken jar. Each pulse of the Heart's glow was dimmer than the last, the threads holding him aloft fraying and snapping one by one. The man wasn't more than a shade now, his skin nearly translucent and his bones sharp beneath it, his eyes shut as though he'd already let go.

It wasn't until that moment that Thane finally listened... finally understood. If Echo finished, if he siphoned and emptied the Heart completely, Arbelon would fall. And Lirien would die—the last person he had left to fight for would be gone.

Something shifted inside him. A soundless surge, a rage, but orderly, cutting through the growing static in his mind.

It was the nanovirions. They rose like a tide beneath his skin, millions of silver mites spinning in tight orbits through his veins. They had no words and were relentless

—just a pressure in his skull, a direction burned into instinct. He could feel their network latching onto the lattice, into the Heart, into *him*.

They offered him only one path. More of an in-line command of code that somehow he understood.

Reverse magic. Kill source. Kill Heart.

He swayed on his knees, blood dripping onto the glitching stones below him. Lirien's face flashed in his mind, her eyes wide, mouth shaping his name through the distortion. The next image was his father's, smiling, years ago, before the disease and the nanovirions... before the Heart.

Thane closed his eyes.

"I'm sorry," he whispered, voice trembling. "But if I don't... we all die."

His hands rose, his fingers splayed toward the glowing threads that connected Heart to lattice, and the lattice to world. They shimmered like cords of spun glass, impossibly delicate. He gripped them in his mind, and pulled.

The current shuddered, then faltered, and then began to reverse, the light draining back into him. For a heartbeat, he saw the lattice not as vines or light, but as an endless web of pulsing code, every strand a string of symbols burning away as Thane pulled harder, tightening his grip.

The nanovirions screamed through his blood, not with sound but with heat, every synapse igniting until it felt like his bones were molten metal. They fused with the flow, turning it crimson-gold, feeding on the raw energy and driving it backward through the lattice.

The air around him stuttered, frames of the world skipping, like a memory played too fast then too slow. The edges of the glade warped inward, the trees bowing toward him as though gravity had shifted. The Heart convulsed in its cradle, and the glade quaked. The sky above the glade pixelated, breaking into jagged shards of night and pale daylight, before snapping back together with a sound like tearing denim.

Spiderweb fractures spread through the cords under his grip, and something in the womb tore loose. It was a sound like a shattering star had ripped through the glade, and the world's breath rushed inward—into him.

The womb ruptured in a flare of gold and shadow, its lattice exploding outward in a rain of fractal light. Magic poured into him, but not just magic, his father's life force, the raw, wild core of Arbelon itself. It hit like molten metal flooding his veins, searing, uncontainable.

His eyes blazed white, and his veins lit as if carved from lightning, pulsing with every frantic beat of his heart. The nanovirions screamed in unison inside him, their voices a chorus of agony and exaltation, binding him to every thread of the realm.

Echo froze, his outline splitting into jagged doubles as he glitched so violently the air itself tore. His eyes were wide in disbelief, and his lips parted to speak, but the words never came.

Thane screamed, and the sound was not his own. It was the roar of oceans, the cry of mountains breaking, and the blast that followed was beyond magic—it was a wild nova, an unchained cataclysm.

Light tore through the glade in a perfect sphere, not shredding it to ash, but peeling it open. Bark sloughed away to reveal lattices of living light, branches mapped in shifting lines of code that pulsed like veins. The stone underfoot dissolved into translucent polygons, flickering in and out of solid form before re-skinning itself in moss and lichen.

Above, the sky inverted—daylight bleeding into

starlight in a single breath—then fractured into cascading auroras. In their glow, the air itself seemed written, lines of alien script rippling past as though the world was a page being turned.

For an instant, everything was naked—raw framework and fractured geometry, the truth beneath the beauty—before the polished veneer rushed back, hiding it all once more.

Echo's body came apart mid-glitch, pixel by pixel, the static of his frame stretching into nothing. By the time the blast faded, nothing remained but a heap of fine black ash, and the Heart's cradle hung empty. His father's body dropped from the torn womb, weightless and fragile.

Thane lunged, hands closing around him… only for the body to crumble into golden sand, scattering through Thane's fingers, a fine dust drifting upward in a slow, spiraling column, catching on stray beams of light from the reformed canopy. For a heartbeat, the dust shaped the outline of his father's face, his eyes warm, proud, before scattering into the wind.

And then it was gone.

Thane fell to his knees, his wound knitted by the magic. Around him, the glade dimmed, the magic receding like a tide pulling away from shore. Shadows lengthened, settling into the hollow spaces left behind, into the spaces where shadows were meant to live.

The truth of the moment hit like a blade to the chest. He was alone. His mother gone. His father gone. Whatever he'd taken in, whatever he'd done, it hadn't brought them back.

The silence after the nova was worse than the blast.

The glade sagged, as if the magic holding it upright had been cut loose. Vines slumped from the Womb, their once-luminous veins dulled to brittle gray. The lattice that had cradled the Heart folded inward like a dying star, each segment flickering out until nothing but shadow remained.

The light bled away. Not slowly, it was like someone had reached up and dimmed the sun in one twist.

Lirien hit the ground hard, freed from Echo's coils. She rolled to her side, coughing, her breath clouding in the sudden cold. When she looked up, her eyes locked on Thane's. She didn't speak. She didn't have to. The shock, the gratitude, the dawning horror—they were all there in the space between them.

Behind her, the Womb was empty. The Heart was gone. And with it, the pulse that had kept Arbelon alive, and Thane could feel it in his bones. The air was thinner, and the ground trembled in slow, unsteady breaths. Somewhere far off, a sound like tearing cloth moved through the world.

Arbelon was dying.

The collapse shuddered through the glade, but Thane barely felt it. Every step toward Lirien came heavier, the glitches rippling through his body now—whole pieces of him phasing in and out, like he was already half-remembered.

"Thane—" Lirien's voice cracked as she staggered to meet him. She grabbed his hands, holding on like she could anchor him here by will alone. "You can't leave me. Not again—"

He reached up, brushing the back of his fingers along her cheek. The warmth of her skin was the last real thing he wanted to feel.

"I came back for you," he said, voice rough but certain. "To save you. And to make right what I stole from you."

Her breath caught. She kissed him—hard and desperate—and he kissed her. No words could have carried the weight between them.

When she pulled back, her eyes flicked to the Womb. The core still glowed, but faintly, its light already bleeding out into the dying air. Around them, the world glitched harder now, its edges folding, it colors draining, and the ground beneath them trembled like it couldn't decide whether to exist.

Then Lirien started to wink in and out, like a scene dissolving before his eyes.

It was at that moment he knew what he had to do.

"There's still one last chance…" Thane whispered.

Her grip on his hands tightened, as if she knew the answer as certain as he did. "No. You can't—"

He cupped her face again, thumb brushing away a tear.

"It's the Final Save."

She shook her head, but he was already stepping away. Each pace toward the empty cradle felt like it stripped something from him. When he reached it, the vines stirred, reaching out, like they had been waiting. They unfurled with slow, deliberate grace, curling around his arms, his chest, his legs. They didn't drag him in. They welcomed him. Almost instantly, the light returned, but it wasn't wild this time. It was gentle and steady. There was a warmth that chased the cold from the air.

Lirien's voice broke across the distance between them. "Thane—please—"

He met her eyes, and for the first time in a long time, he smiled. Then the vines drew him into the Womb, and his shape began to dissolve—not fading, not dying, but becoming light.

His light began as a single thread from the Womb— thin, golden, and impossibly pure. Then it widened, spilling out in waves that rolled through the glade, but it didn't burn or roar. It was warm and gentle. The kind of light you could rest in forever.

The vines that had gone slack now stirred, blooming in slow, unhurried unfurls—petals opening like they'd been holding their breath for years, waiting for him. The lattice knitted itself back together, each strand catching the light like spun glass. The air shimmered, not with heat, but with life—soft, overlapping notes, a chorus without a source, as if the whole world was singing.

Lirien dropped to her knees. Her hands shook as she reached out to the base of the Heart. The vines there shifted, curling tenderly around her fingers, warm and alive. Her lips trembled, and a tear slipped free, falling onto the living green.

"You did it," she whispered.

The glitches were gone. The jagged edges of the world smoothed away, and Arbelon exhaled, slow and whole again.

She stayed there, head bowed, her hair falling like a curtain to hide the tears she didn't bother to stop. It wasn't the joy she'd imagined. It was joy with an empty place carved into it.

Still, she held on to the vines, letting their warmth anchor her in the quiet.

20

____

WHAT REMAINS

She came alone and the world offered no name for the place.

Grass, short and wind-bruised, tilted and straightened again around her ankles. The light had that washed, late-day patience that could belong to any sky. Far off, something called once and fell quiet, but the sound carried clean and thin, like a memory stretched across water.

Her face stayed in the shade of a hood, or maybe it was only the way the light refused her. What showed of her was simple: a hand at her side, the hem of a dark coat, the slow bookkeeping of breath in cold air. In the other hand, a single flower—nondescript and stubbornly ordinary, but beautiful. Its petals caught the sun and held it for a heartbeat longer than they should have. Or perhaps it didn't. It was hard to tell.

She walked the small distance without hurry. The wind moved when she did, then seemed to think better of it and lagged a step behind. Shadows kept neat edges. Nothing creaked and nothing broke.

The marker waited in a shallow dip of ground. There

was no fence or path, just a stone worn down to its own idea of shape, lichen stippled along the face like old ash. It could have been dragged here from a field, or left behind when the field forgot itself.

She stopped.

For a moment, the world hesitated—sun, wind, the soft stitch of sound—and then carried on as if nothing had paused at all.

She lowered to one knee, slow, careful. Up close, the stone showed its years: hairline cracks fanned from a corner, moss pressed into them like ink in a letter that had been read too often. There were no dates, and no epitaph. No emblem to explain itself.

Only the name, cut clean and shallow:

THANE THOMAS ASH

Nothing else.

She stayed there for a long moment, as if deciding whether to move at all.

Then the flower shifted in her hand, petals trembling against the wind, and she leaned forward. The stone took the offering without comment. The stem lay against the lichen, green against gray, a single thread of color in the weathered face. She let her fingers rest at the base for a moment before tracing upward, slow, deliberate, until they found the name.

The carved letters were shallow now—worn by years, or rain, or some other, older weather. Her thumb followed each one, memorizing its shape.

She bent her head. The hood hid her face, but a drop of water fell to the stone, soaking into the moss, and another followed.

"I remember," she said. Barely more than breath. It

was not clear whether she was speaking to him, or to herself.

The air shifted in answer. A breeze, gentle and almost warm, passed over her shoulders. Or maybe it was only the way the world sometimes moves when no one's watching.

For a while, she didn't move.

The wind passed once more, stirring the grass around her knees, bending it in a slow ripple that carried outward until it vanished.

The world beyond was still, unmarked, as if it had nothing to add.

The light shifted on the stone, catching on the etched letters. The wind let go. The grass settled.

Just the stone, the flower, the wind—and the woman. A small shape beside a nameless marker in a field without a map.

He was gone. And still—he remained.

ENJOYED THE FINAL SAVE?

Thanks for sticking with Thane to the end. *The Final Save* brings the Broken Circle Duology to its close with the same mix of grit, magic, and ambiguity that it began with. If the story moved you, puzzled you, or stuck with you, I'd be grateful if you left a short review.

The Broken Circle may be complete, but the journey isn't over. New stories are already stirring and being written, and you can get a first look at them by subscribing on *detect magic*.

Subscribe at - https://danblakely.substack.com/

Books by Dan Blakely

The Fall of Fate Duology
- The Last Gambler*
- Pieces of Eight

The Broken Circle Duology
  • No Extra Lives
  • The Final Save

*Read Ch. 1 from *The Last Gambler* in the following pages.

ABOUT THE AUTHOR

My journey started in a sleepy Midwestern town in the summer of 1971, pretty much at the dawn of all that was to be awesome in the world. I still remember watching Star Wars erupt on the world and the late nights playing D&D. Like a gaggle of other kids, that's where my love for fantasy stories took root. I grew up on Tolkien and Donaldson and Moorcock and Herbert and more. Sure, I played soccer and hung out with friends, but I was always looking for fantasy stories to devour. It didn't matter if it was a book, comic, movie, magazine or video game (even Zork!). The endless worlds and stories the human mind can imagine remain irresistible. There's nothing quite like strolling through a freshly created world—simply magical.

Before landing in California, I bounced around from coast to coast. Along the way, my love for fantasy never left. I've always kept journals and notes of ideas. Over the past few years, I've been weaving stories using those ideas to create worlds and the people living in them. I want to introduce you to people and worlds that inspire you, perhaps even surprise you. Hopefully, after meeting them and living in their worlds, you'll long for more, always wondering what happens next. Maybe their stories will even change you along the way. Oh, and of course, a little magic in a story is always a good thing.

If you'd like to read more or stay up to date on new releases, you can find me at:

www.DanBlakely.com
https://danblakely.substack.com/

And if you enjoyed this book, I'd be grateful for a short review on the page where you bought it. Reviews make a huge difference in helping new readers discover these stories.

The last thing I'd ask is simple: if this book spoke to you, please share it with one other person. Referrals are the lifeblood of stories, and I'd be honored if I've earned that from you.

Thank You!

ACKNOWLEDGMENTS

Thanks to my family, friends, and the *detect magic* readers who've been part of this journey from the very beginning. Publishing a book is never a solitary act—it truly does take a village. With your encouragement, feedback, and belief, we made it not just to the finish line of a single story, but to the close of this duology.

And to you, the reader: thank you for walking beside Thane all the way through *No Extra Lives* and now *The Final Save*. Without you, these worlds would remain only in my head, scribbles in a notebook. Because of you, they came alive. If the Broken Circle left its mark, even in some small way, then every word was worth writing.

READY FOR MORE?

The Broken Circle Duology has come to its end, but another path awaits…

On the following pages, you'll find Chapter One of **The Last Gambler***, the opening to my other duology, The Fall of Fate.*

If it speaks to you, I'd be grateful to have you along for that adventure too.

Let's jump in…

CHAPTER 1

THE BLACK HOUSE

The darkness wrapped around Rye like a cloak, creating a sense of unease. She fixed her gaze on the narrow path winding through the woods ahead, leading her deeper into the forest. The creek, a ribbon of silver in the gloom, tracked alongside it. She'd thought herself clever, masking her tracks with care, but the sweat on her brow and the pounding of her heart told otherwise. Glancing over her shoulder, she quickened her pace, her footfalls hitting the ground with a soft thud, muffling any betrayal of her presence. As the trail curved closer to the creek, the gentle rush of water cascading over rocks whispered to her, but she ignored it. Her every nerve was stretched taut, every sense on alert for the slightest hint of pursuit. In the darkness, there were only two options: hide, or be hunted.

Her eyes darted about frantically, scouring the woods ahead for somewhere to hide, but the trees were thick, obscuring everything in shadows. Anger burned deep within as she pushed herself harder, faster along the twisting trail. *Why can't they just let me be?* Rye thought bitterly, her attention wandering. She returned her focus to the trail a moment too late, her foot catching on an exposed tree root. She stumbled, arms flailing to catch her fall, but her momentum sent her tumbling off the trail. Unable to regain her footing, she slid down the hillside and gracelessly crashed through the underbrush to the creek below. She gasped in surprise as the icy water splashed up her leg, flooding her shoes.

"Son of a bitch!" she cursed, momentarily surrendering her stealth, but she hated having wet feet. On top of that, she'd now left a trail that anyone could follow. Thankfully, a glance back up the hill revealed nothing, only the redwoods towering above her. She took a minute to collect her thoughts and rest. Her breath came in quick wisps, leaving ghosts drifting through the air before they faded away in the moonlight. Craning her neck, she sniffed the air, still learning to use her heightened senses. They were getting closer. Two against one—not good odds, even for her.

Pulling her grey stocking cap on tighter, she took a deep breath. *It'll be okay. Just keep moving,* she reassured herself. They'd played this game of cat and mouse over a dozen times in the past few years. She'd always been the mouse, always running, and they weren't far behind now. Turning back, she looked at the creek. The light of the moon reflected off the surface of the water, revealing its meandering path through the trees. She stepped out of the cool water onto a wide trail on the opposite bank and pressed onward, but her feet were now freezing, water squishing out with every step.

Around a bend in the trail, she suddenly caught the dull glint of metal in the moonlight. Whatever it was, she'd learned to keep a wary eye out when *they* were following her. She slowed her pace, inching forward until she could make out an ornate iron gate attached to two large redwoods flanking the trail. The gate stood taller than Rye, one side hanging off its hinges in obvious disrepair. Above the gate, an iron sign stretched between the trees, adorned with simple white block letters: *Black Creek Cemetery, 1889*.

Beyond the gate, a ghostly sheen of moonlight filtered through the trees, revealing a wide clearing pockmarked with a hodgepodge of gravestones of various sizes. The cemetery was overgrown with tall grasses and periwinkle, and a reluctant fog hugged the ground, casting awkward shadows all around. Stepping up to the gate, Rye shivered. This place looked gloomier the closer she came, and one never knew what might be lurking in the shadows.

Her hand froze as she tentatively reached out to open the gate. "Shit," she breathed. She took a small step backwards, tightening her jacket, then glanced behind herself. The thought of going into a creepy cemetery in the dead of night was almost too much. Her eyes searched for another passage, but the trail ended here. *Just keep moving.* That simple mantra pulled her forward. She reached out, pushing the gate open, going rigid as it let out a metallic shriek from years of neglect, echoing through the trees, shattering the silence. Her heart pounded, and again she turned, looking behind herself. Nothing. But it wouldn't be that way for long—not now. She had to keep moving.

Not wanting to risk any further noise, she squeezed her body through the narrow opening in the gate. Moving from gravestone to gravestone, she cautiously picked her way across the cemetery, trying to stay hidden. Suddenly, the telltale shriek of the gate sounded again, and she ducked behind a large tomb. Silence. Crouching down, she wiped the sweat from her brow, straining her ears for any sound.

"Hey, little magpie," a warm voice with a Southern drawl called out from the darkness.

Rye tensed. Liora was toying with her. Rye peered around the tomb, holding her breath. Liora wore an immaculate cream trench coat, and even in the dark, she sported her signature rhinestone-studded Dolce & Gabbana sunglasses. She had an uncanny way of sweet-talking people, spreading a bit of hope just before the hammer dropped. The hammer, of course, was her partner, Ciara, her opposite in all ways. Ciara dressed all in black leathers, blending with her jet-black eyes, and she was nothing short of dark and disturbing. Together, they made a frightful pair, even to Rye, and they knew she hated being called "magpie." She'd pleaded with the Lady to pick something different, but the Lady had held fast, calling the members of the Sorority her "flock."

Another screech of the gate, and it banged closed a moment later. Rye swore under her breath.

"I know you're out there," Liora called. "You can stop running if you just give us the necklace. I'm sure we could come to an arrangement—one that ensures your safety. Then you can go off with that sweaty boyfriend of yours, make some pups, live the good life." Liora's voice was gentle, almost pleasant, but it was much closer than Rye preferred.

Rye scoffed, almost giving away her position. She wanted nothing to do with Noah—not after what he'd done to her. She'd made that clear to him before she left him. Still, she'd grown weary of running. *Maybe there really is a workable arrangement*, she thought, the possibilities swirling in her head. That is, until Ciara chimed in.

"You can't leave the Sorority, and you certainly can't steal from it," Ciara said. "That's not how it works. You know that." Unlike Liora's somewhat melodic voice,

Ciara's was like gravel in a wooden bucket, raspy and harsh. And unlike with Liora, kind words were not a gift Ciara possessed nor enjoyed. Instead, she opted to be direct, often employing threats to make her point.

Rye's face flushed, and she clenched her fists. It took everything she could muster to not yell out in protest. *The Sorority.* She sneered. She hadn't asked to be part of it, but Ciara was right: once you were marked, you could never leave it. So, she'd run, leaving that world behind. And stealing? She resented the accusation. She hadn't stolen a damn thing. The necklace they hunted—she'd earned it for her years of service. Why else would the Lady have left it out the night Rye fled with Noah? Little happened by chance when it came to the Lady. Rye remained convinced it was a gift, and she didn't like being called a thief, especially by Ciara, of all people. They were goading her, and she couldn't believe that she'd almost considered an *arrangement* with them.

She leaned her back against the cool stone, taking a settling breath. Listening for footsteps, she heard nothing. Even the crickets were now silent as an unnatural stillness descended on the cemetery. Wispy tendrils of fog worked their way through the treetops, and the stars were disappearing one by one, as if a blanket were being pulled across the sky. Within moments, the fog had obscured everything in the sky, swallowing up even the moon. Only darkness remained. That was what Ciara preferred. Rye had seen Ciara call the darkness before, but never this fast. She was getting stronger.

Rye slowed her breath, sharpening her focus. In the past, she would've felt vulnerable in the dark, but Noah had changed that. He claimed he'd given her a gift, but it wasn't; it was a curse that she'd never wanted. In fact, he'd agreed to never visit it upon her. His failure to keep that promise was the final blow, driving a wedge deep between them. At the moment, however, his "gift" was proving useful. The shadows and shapes in the distance were unnaturally distinct, and Rye could even see Liora and Ciara at the gate, watching. The forest beyond the cemetery was visible as well, and she spied what looked like a faded game trail. That would have to do.

Just keep moving, she repeated, but then a sudden chill breeze kissed her cheek. She grasped her jacket, pulling it around herself even tighter. The air around her had turned frigid, her breath prominent even in the gloom as a sheen of frost suddenly formed on the surrounding ground. A cool gust passed through her hair from behind, and goose bumps pricked her skin in warning. She spun around, seeing a shadow shift in the darkness before her. Whatever it was, it remained hidden in the mists. *This is precisely why I don't like cemeteries.* She'd heard stories about things that lived in graveyards, but it was unsettling to experience it in person. She searched the darkness for the shadow, glimpsing it again before something resolved in the distance. A smile touched her lips. Tucked into the woods, a small, dark house was hidden in the fog. This had to be her escape.

Bending over, Rye picked up a baseball-sized chunk of stone fallen from one of the crumbling gravestones. With all her strength, she wound up, lobbing the rock through the air toward the faded trail she'd seen on the edge of the woods. With a loud thud, the rock landed, crashing into a fallen branch and rolling through the underbrush before coming to a stop beside the trail. Rye crouched in silence, listening, hoping it was enough to bait them.

Ciara and Liora were arguing, but a moment later, the crunch of leaves confirmed that they were on the move. A final peek revealed their silhouettes moving through the gravestones toward the faded trail. Rye held her position, watching as they leaped the fence and continued down the trail before disappearing into the forest.

Still crouching, she picked her way across the cemetery, careful to stay hidden. Even though she could no longer see them, their scent hung heavy in the air, an unsettling mixture of flowers and rot. Luckily for Rye, their scent was fading. As she crept closer, the little house revealed itself. It was painted black, almost invisible in the darkness. It was smaller than she'd expected, but it would do. A chimney towered above the roof. The shutters were closed, but the front door stood ajar. The scent of mothballs and mildew wafted out, overwhelming her senses. That same strange stirring in the darkness pulled her forward, goose bumps once again peppering her skin. The open door revealed little. Inside, all was an inky black, with no beginning or end.

She knew they would expect her to run, just like last time at the music festival in Cologne, and the carnival in Lisbon before that. Cat and mouse, ad nauseam. But this time would be different. She took one last look behind her before squeezing through the doorway, careful to close the door quietly behind her.

Unlike outside, the inky blackness of the shuttered house was complete. She couldn't even see her own hand as she waved it in front of her face. She spread her arms, searching for the wall. Her fingers found the smooth wood, and she followed it, circling the room. A stone fireplace came first, followed by a few of the shuttered windows and another door. She settled into a corner, sitting with her back to the wall, careful not to get too comfortable, even though she was wet and cold. She'd slipped past them again. The darkness swam about her, and she thought of the shadow in the graveyard, wondering if she was alone.

"Thank you for your help," she whispered into the darkness, not wanting a good deed to go unrecognized. No response came. She let out a deep sigh, grateful for the silence.

Time moved like molasses dripping from a spoon, and she did her best to stay alert. She'd already recited the lyrics of her favorite songs a hundred times and had just started naming all the subway stations in London. Her attention waned as her head drooped, and her body slumped forward before she caught herself. She refocused, slapping her own face and starting on the subway stations again, still drifting in and out.

… until she startled to the sound of a door closing.

Shit! She wasn't sure if she'd dozed off and just imagined the sound. Dark places could mask the truth, and this room was awash in it, the pungent scent of mothballs suffocating her senses. Her heart raced as adrenaline surged through her veins. Closing her eyes, she took a calming breath, trying to convince herself that she'd imagined the noise, but it was too late. A bit of fear had seeped in, and she knew where that would lead.

A moment later, Liora's sweet voice washed in from outside the front door.

"No need to cower in a dingy old caretaker's house, little magpie," Liora called. "You're better than this. Just give us the necklace, and I'm sure we can work something out."

Rye stared into the darkness as a switch flipped inside her, taking hold of her blood. Only one word came to mind: *Run.* Before she knew it, she'd crashed into the back door, grabbing the handle and trying to open it, but it didn't budge. Blood pounded in her head as she moved to the window, throwing her body into it, but it held firm too. The mixture of fear and adrenaline had taken over, and the darkness seemed to deepen, closing its noose around her.

"You having some problems with the door?" Liora asked in that sweet voice. "Funny thing. The old caretaker was so afraid of the creatures of the night…" She rapped her knuckles on the front door. "Hear that? Rowan. He built this entire cabin out of rowan wood. You know, to keep certain things out—or *in*, in your case. Just so happens you stumbled upon the worst possible place to hide. Amazing, really, if you think of the possibilities. So, what do you say—ready to make that deal?"

Rye leaned her forehead against the wall. She couldn't believe it. She'd trapped herself. Her thoughts flashed back to the shadow in the cemetery, hearing her mother's voice chiding her. *"Be wary of the things in the darkness. They often wish us harm."* So true, but unfortunately in hindsight. Out of habit, her hand moved to her chest, reaching for her necklace, but she already knew it wasn't there. Noah had stolen it. That's what had caused their breakup—that and his bite, which now left her trapped. There was no deal to be made with these ladies—not tonight or any other night. The only thing left was to fight.

"No? That's most unfortunate," Liora said.

A moment later, Ciara let out a shrill cackle from *inside* the house. A shiver coursed down Rye's spine, but she stood tall, ready for whatever would come next. She winced as her bones cracked and stretched, the hair on her skin filling out into a plush pelt. The change was still new to her. She found it unsettling, but she'd managed it before. She turned her body toward where Ciara's voice had been.

Too late. Ciara's face illuminated in the eerie glow of electricity arcing from a cattle prod she pressed into Rye's belly. In an instant, the adrenaline drained from Rye's body, and the burgeoning changes dissipated, along with any chance of her escaping this time. She fell to the floor, her body convulsing, as Ciara stood above her, releasing the button.

"You'd better hope you kill me," Rye said through gritted teeth, the scent of burnt flesh saturating the air.

"You only wish it'd be that quick," Ciara said from the darkness.

Rye recoiled as the metal rod pressed against her chest, followed by a subtle click. The blueish-white glow raged again, reflected on Ciara's sneering face. Something cold fastened around her neck, and then she blacked out.

www.ingramcontent.com/pod-product-compliance
Lightning Source LLC
Chambersburg PA
CBHW032255310726
48973CB00008B/2421